THE DOCKYARD ORPHAN OF STORMY WEYMOUTH

RACHEL DOWNING

CORNERSTONETALES.COM

PART I
THE ORPHAN OF WEYMOUTH

1855-1859

MORNING FOG AND FRESH BREAD

The fog rolled in from the sea, blanketing Weymouth in a soft, eerie grey. Light from the rising sun struggled to penetrate the dense mist, casting a muted glow over the cobblestone streets.

Sarah Campbell stood on her tiptoes — as tall as her small nine year old legs could take her — straining to see over the windowsill of her family's bakery. Her light blue eyes, wide with curiosity, peered through the fog-shrouded street. The mist clung to everything, transforming familiar buildings into looming shadows.

She spotted her father's figure disappearing into the grey haze. His broad shoulders were hunched against the morning chill as he strode purposefully towards the railway construction site. Sarah's small hands pressed against the cool glass, leaving ghostly imprints as condensation formed around her fingers.

"Papa," she whispered, her breath fogging the window.

The scent of fresh bread filled the air, mingling with the damp earthiness seeping in from outside. Sarah inhaled deeply, savouring the comforting aroma that always reminded her of home and family.

She heard her mother bustling about in the kitchen, preparing Papa's lunch for the day. The familiar sounds of pots clanking and bread being wrapped in paper drifted through the bakery.

Sarah's heart fluttered with a mixture of excitement as she watched her father's familiar form recede into the mist. She pressed her nose against the cool glass, leaving a small smudge, her eyes never leaving the spot where he'd disappeared.

"Sarah, love, come away from the window," her mother called from the kitchen. "You'll catch a chill."

With a small sigh, Sarah reluctantly stepped back, her bare feet padding softly on the worn wooden floor. She turned towards the warm glow of the kitchen, where her mother stood kneading dough, her arms dusted with flour.

"Come now," her mother said, gesturing with flour-covered hands. "Help me shape these loaves. We've got a busy day ahead."

Sarah moved to join her mother, standing on her tiptoes to reach the countertop. As she worked the dough with small, determined hands, her thoughts drifted back to her father. She pictured him at the railway site, strong and capable, helping to build something grand and exciting.

A sudden gust of wind rattled the shop's sign outside, drawing Sarah's attention back to the window. The fog seemed to have thickened, transforming the street into a dreamlike landscape. For a moment, Sarah imagined she could still see her father's silhouette in the distance.

Then, as if sensing her gaze, Thomas Campbell's figure emerged briefly from the mist. He glanced back towards the bakery, his weathered face breaking into a warm smile as he raised his hand in a reassuring wave. Sarah's heart swelled with love and pride.

Her father adjusted his flat cap, tucking away the strands of salt-and-pepper hair that had escaped in the damp air. With one last look, he turned and strode purposefully back into the fog, his broad shoulders soon swallowed by the grey veil.

Sarah strained her ears, listening to the fading sound of her father's heavy boots on the cobblestones. The rhythmic footfalls grew fainter and fainter until they were replaced by the distant clatter of horse-drawn carts, muffled by the thick mist.

Sarah turned away from the window. The warmth from the ovens enveloped her, chasing away the chill that had seeped into her bones while watching her father disappear into the fog.

Inside, her mother, Agatha Campbell, bustled about with practiced efficiency. Her apron was already dusted with flour, testament to the early morning's work. Sarah watched, mesmerised, as her mother's hands moved with grace and purpose, kneading dough and shaping loaves.

"Come, my little gift," Agatha called, her voice as warm as the ovens surrounding them. "Help me pack your father's lunch."

Sarah eagerly joined her mother at the worn wooden table. Agatha carefully selected thick slices of homemade bread, still warm from the oven. The crusty exterior gave way to a soft, pillowy interior as she arranged them on a clean cloth.

"Now, what else should we add?" Agatha asked, her eyes twinkling with affection.

"Cheese!" Sarah exclaimed, reaching for a wedge of sharp cheddar. "And an apple, Papa's favourite."

Agatha nodded approvingly, her smile crinkling the corners of her eyes. "That's right, love. Your father works so hard; we must make sure he has a good meal to keep him strong."

As they worked together, the aroma of freshly baked bread filled the small, warmly lit bakery. It mingled with the smell of yeast and sugar, creating a symphony of comforting smells that Sarah associated with home and love. She inhaled deeply, savouring the familiar fragrance.

"Mama," Sarah said, her voice tinged with curiosity, "will you take Papa his lunch today?"

Agatha paused in her wrapping, considering the question. "I think I shall, dear heart. It's been a while since I've visited the railway site, and I'd like to see how the work is progressing."

Sarah's eyes lit up at the prospect of visiting the railway site. Her heart raced with excitement as she imagined the bustling activity, the gleaming rails, and the towering machines that her father had described. The construction site had always held a mysterious allure for her, a place where dreams of progress and adventure seemed to come alive.

She turned to her mother, her small hands clasped together in anticipation. "Mother," Sarah began, her voice brimming with hope, "may I go with you to see Father and the railway?"

Sarah watched as her mother's expression softened, a familiar mix of love and gentle firmness settling across her features. Agatha's hands, still dusted with flour, paused in their work as she considered her daughter's request.

"Not today, my dear," Agatha said, her tone kind but resolute. "There is much to be done here, and I need your help."

Sarah's heart sank, disappointment clouding her face like the fog outside. She had so hoped to see the marvels her father spoke of, to breathe in the excitement of progress and change. For a moment, she wanted to protest, to plead her case, but the sense of responsibility instilled in her by her parents won out.

With a small sigh, Sarah nodded reluctantly. "Yes, Mother," she said, her voice quiet but steady. She understood the importance of her duties at the bakery, the need to contribute to the family's livelihood.

Sarah's disappointment lingered for a moment, but she pushed it aside, focusing instead on the tasks at hand. The bakery was her home, filled with warmth and the comforting scents of fresh bread and pastries. She knew every nook and cranny, every utensil and ingredient, and took pride in her growing skills.

Agatha smiled softly at her daughter's resilience. "Come now, let's get you ready for the day's work."

Sarah nodded, her spirits lifting as she moved to fetch her small apron from its hook, a familiar routine. She carefully looped the apron strings around her waist, her small fingers working deftly to tie a neat bow at the back.

As she smoothed down the front of her apron, Sarah felt the rough texture of the fabric beneath her palms. It was worn soft in places from years of use, carrying the history of countless loaves and pastries. The apron had been her mother's when she was a girl, passed down like a cherished heirloom.

Once Sarah was properly attired, Agatha beckoned her over to the large wooden worktable. A substantial ball of dough sat waiting, its pale surface dusted with a fine layer of flour.

"Watch closely, love," Agatha instructed, her hands moving with practiced grace. She pressed her palms into the dough, pushing it away before folding it back on itself. The motions were fluid and rhythmic, almost hypnotic.

Sarah observed intently, marvelling at the way the dough transformed under her mother's expert touch. It seemed to come alive, stretching and folding with each movement.

After a few moments of demonstration, Agatha stepped back. "Now you try, Sarah. Remember, gentle but firm. Let the dough guide your hands."

With a small hint of trepidation, Sarah approached the worktable. She stood on her tiptoes, reaching out to place her small hands on the cool, sticky mass. The dough yielded beneath her touch, soft yet resistant.

Sarah began to knead, mimicking her mother's movements. She pushed the dough away, then pulled it back, feeling it stretch and compress beneath her fingers. The rhythmic motion was soothing, and she found herself falling into a steady pattern.

As she worked, a connection built within Sarah – to her mother, to the bakery, to the generations of bakers who had come before. Her small hands moved with increasing confidence, shaping the dough that would soon become nourishing bread for their customers.

As Sarah's small hands worked the dough, she felt a sense of pride growing within her. The sticky mass was slowly transforming under her touch, becoming smoother and more malleable with each push and fold. She glanced up at her mother, seeking approval, and was rewarded with a warm smile that made her heart swell.

Agatha began to hum softly as she moved about the bakery, preparing for the day ahead. The melody was familiar to Sarah, a gentle tune that her mother often sang at bedtime. It floated through the air, mingling with the comforting scents of yeast and warm bread.

Sarah closed her eyes for a moment, letting the sound wash over her. The notes seemed to weave themselves into the very fabric of the bakery, becoming part of the morning ritual. She found herself swaying slightly as she worked, her movements falling into rhythm with her mother's humming.

The familiar tune transported Sarah back to cosy evenings spent curled up in her bed, listening to her mother's soothing voice as she drifted off to sleep. Now, in the early morning light, it felt like a warm embrace, chasing away any lingering sleepiness and filling her with a sense of security.

As she continued to knead, Sarah became aware of the stark contrast between the warmth of the bakery and the chill that seeped in from outside. The fog still clung to the windows, transforming the street beyond into a mysterious, grey world. But inside, everything was golden and warm, filled with the promise of fresh bread and the comfort of family.

As Sarah finished kneading the dough, her small arms aching pleasantly from the effort, she stepped back to admire her handiwork. The once sticky mass had transformed into a smooth, elastic ball under her careful ministrations. Accomplishment swelled in her as she watched her mother gently lift the dough and place it in a large bowl, covering it with a damp cloth to rise.

"Well done, my little gift," Agatha said, her voice warm with pride. "God's given you quite the touch for baking."

Sarah beamed at the praise, her cheeks flushing with pleasure. She dusted the flour from her hands, leaving small white handprints on her apron. As her mother moved to tend to the ovens, Sarah found herself drawn back to the window.

The fog still hung heavy over Weymouth, transforming the familiar streets into a mysterious landscape. Sarah pressed her nose against the cool glass, her breath creating small patches of condensation. Her eyes strained to pierce the grey veil, imagining the railway construction site hidden somewhere beyond.

In her mind's eye, Sarah could see the bustle of activity her father had described. She pictured towering cranes reaching into the sky, their metal arms swinging to and fro as they lifted heavy loads. She imagined the rhythmic clanging of hammers on metal, the hiss of steam engines, and the shouts of workers coordinating their efforts.

Sarah's imagination painted a vivid picture of men in dusty clothes and flat caps, much like her father's, scurrying about like ants on a great mound. In her fantasy, she could almost feel the rumble of the earth as massive machines carved out the path for the railway tracks.

The young girl's thoughts drifted to the trains themselves. She had seen pictures in books, but to see one in person, to hear its whistle and feel the rush of wind as it sped by – the very idea made her heart race with excitement. Sarah wondered how the railway would change their little town of Weymouth. Would it bring new faces, new stories from far-off places?

Sarah watched as her mother carefully wrapped the last slice of bread in a clean cloth, tucking it into the basket alongside the cheese and apple.

Agatha moved towards the door, her steps purposeful yet unhurried. She reached for the worn wool shawl that hung from a hook nearby, its familiar weave speaking of countless journeys through Weymouth's unpredictable weather. With practiced ease, she draped it over her shoulders.

Sarah's eyes followed her mother's movements, a mix of emotions swirling within her. Part of her still longed to accompany Agatha to the construction site, to see the marvels her father spoke of with such enthusiasm. Yet she understood her place was here, tending to the bakery.

Agatha turned back to Sarah, her eyes softening as they met her daughter's. She bent down, her face level with Sarah's, and placed a gentle kiss on the girl's forehead. The familiar scent of flour and vanilla enveloped Sarah.

"Be good, Sarah," Agatha said, her voice warm with affection. "I'll be back soon."

Sarah nodded, straightening her small shoulders as if to show her readiness for the responsibility ahead. She watched as her mother gathered the basket, preparing to step out into the fog-shrouded morning.

Sarah watched as her mother opened the bakery door, letting in a swirl of cool, damp air. The fog seemed to reach its tendrils into the warm sanctuary of the shop, momentarily blurring the line between the cosy interior and the mysterious world beyond. Agatha's figure, wrapped in her familiar shawl, stood silhouetted against the grey backdrop for a moment before she stepped out onto the cobblestones.

"I will be good, Mother," Sarah promised, her voice steady despite the emotions swirling within her.

As the door swung shut behind Agatha, the bell above it giving a final, muted jingle, the bakery's atmosphere shifted. The space seemed larger somehow, emptier without her mother's comforting presence. The hum of the ovens and the lingering scent of fresh bread suddenly felt more pronounced in the quiet.

For a moment, Sarah stood still, her small frame dwarfed by the familiar surroundings that now felt slightly foreign. But then, as if shaking off a spell, she set her jaw with determination. Her mother and father were counting on her, and she would not let them down.

With purposeful steps, Sarah returned to the large wooden worktable. She pulled over the small stool her father had crafted for her, allowing her to reach the tabletop comfortably. Climbing up, she surveyed the array of ingredients before her: flour dusted the surface like a light snowfall, and a large ball of pastry dough sat waiting.

Sarah took a deep breath, inhaling the comforting scents of the bakery. She could almost hear her mother's gentle instructions guiding her actions. With careful movements, she began to roll out the dough, her small hands gripping the wooden rolling pin firmly.

Back and forth she worked, applying gentle pressure as she'd been taught. The dough slowly spread beneath the rolling pin, transforming from a lumpy mass into a smooth, even sheet. Sarah's tongue poked out slightly from the corner of her mouth as she concentrated, determined to achieve the perfect thickness.

As the morning progressed, Sarah managed to settle into a familiar rhythm. The bell above the door chimed, heralding the arrival of their first customer. Mrs Eliza Thompson, shuffled in, her face creasing into a smile as she spotted Sarah behind the counter.

"Good morning, little Miss Campbell," she said. "Where's your mother today?"

Sarah straightened her apron, pushing a stray lock of hair behind her ear. "Good morning, Mrs Thompson. Mother's gone to bring Papa his lunch at the railway site. How may I help you today?"

Mrs Thompson chuckled, her eyes twinkling. "Well, aren't you the proper little shopkeeper? I'll have two of your finest rolls, if you please."

Sarah nodded, her small hands carefully selecting the golden-brown rolls from the display. She wrapped them in brown paper with practiced ease, tying the package with a neat bow of twine. As she handed over the parcel, Mrs Thompson pressed a few coins into her palm.

"Thank you, Mrs Thompson," Sarah said, her voice clear and polite. "I hope you enjoy your breakfast."

As the morning wore on, more customers trickled in. Mr Browning, the owner of the general store, praised Sarah's neat plaits. Mr Heathcliff, the butcher, commented on how she was growing to be the spitting image of her mother. With each interaction, Sarah felt a little taller, a little more confident in her role.

Between customers, Sarah busied herself with the tasks her mother had set out.

Outside, the fog remained thick, transforming Weymouth into a ghostly landscape. But inside the bakery, all was warm and bright. The ovens radiated heat, keeping the chill at bay, while the golden glow of the lamps cast everything in a comforting light.

SHATTERED STILLNESS

Sarah hummed softly to herself as she wiped down the counter, her small hands moving in circular motions across the worn wood. She paused, listening for the distant whistle that would signal the midday break at the railway site, knowing her father would soon be enjoying the lunch her mother had brought him.

The bell above the door chimed, and Sarah looked up to see Mr Finch, the town's postmaster, entering the bakery.

"Good day, Mr Finch," Sarah greeted him. "What can I get for you today?"

Mr Finch startled slightly, as if he'd forgotten where he was. He was a known daydreamer. "Oh, hello there, little Miss Campbell. I'll take a loaf of your father's famous sourdough, if you please."

Sarah nodded, moving to select a perfectly golden loaf from the shelf behind her. She wrapped it carefully in brown paper.

"How is your day going, Mr Finch?" she asked brightly.

The postmaster opened his mouth to reply, but before he could speak, a strange hush fell over the bakery. It was as if all the sounds of the bustling town outside had suddenly been muffled. A chill ran down Sarah's spine, despite the warmth from the ovens.

Then, breaking the eerie silence, came a low, distant rumble. It was unlike anything Sarah had ever heard before – not quite thunder, not quite an explosion. The sound seemed to vibrate through the very foundations of the building.

Mr Finch's face paled. "Good Heavens..." He whispered, his eyes wide with fear.

Sarah moved to the window, standing on her tiptoes to peer out onto the street. She saw people frozen in place, their heads turned towards the outskirts of town where the railway was being built. The fog that had cloaked the morning had lifted somewhat, but a new tension hung in the air, thick and palpable.

Sarah's heart raced as she watched the street through the bakery window. The strange rumble had faded, but its echoes seemed to linger in the air, leaving an unsettling stillness in its wake. She glanced back at Mr Finch, who stood rooted to the spot, his face ashen.

"What was that sound, Mr Finch?" Sarah asked, her voice barely above a whisper.

The postmaster shook his head slowly, his eyes still fixed on the window. "I'm not sure, child, but I fear it's nothing good."

Sarah's mind whirled with possibilities. Had there been an explosion at the railway site? Was her father all right? She longed to run out and find her parents, but she knew she had to mind the bakery. Her mother's words echoed in her ears: "You're in charge while I'm gone, Sarah. Make us proud."

The silence outside was suddenly shattered by the sound of running feet and shouting. Sarah pressed her face against the glass, straining to see what was happening. A figure emerged from the thinning fog, running full tilt down the street. It was a man, his clothes caked with dust and grime, his face a mask of terror.

"Help!" he cried, his voice hoarse and desperate. "There's been a terrible accident at the railway site!"

Sarah's blood ran cold. The railway site – where her father was working, where her mother had gone to bring him lunch. She watched, frozen, as the man's words sent a wave of panic through the townspeople on the street.

Sarah's heart pounded as she watched the panicked man disappear down the street, his cries fading into the distance. She turned to Mr Finch, her eyes wide with fear.

"Mr Finch, I need to go find my parents," she said, her voice trembling.

The postmaster shook his head firmly. "No, Sarah. It's not safe out there."

Sarah bit her lip, torn between her duty and her desperate need to know what had happened. She nodded reluctantly, turning back to the counter.

Mr Finch placed a gentle hand on her shoulder. "I'll go and see what I can find out. You stay here and mind the shop. I'm sure everything will be all right."

As Mr Finch left, the bell above the door chimed softly, Sarah tried to focus on her tasks. She kneaded dough with trembling hands, her mind racing with worry. The bakery felt eerily quiet, the usual chatter of customers replaced by an oppressive silence.

Time seemed to crawl by. Sarah jumped at every sound, hoping it was her parents returning. But the door remained closed, and the street outside grew more frantic with each passing minute.

She could see people hurrying past the window, their faces etched with concern. Some paused to peer inside, their expressions a mixture of pity and sorrow. Sarah's unease grew with each pitying glance.

As she placed a tray of rolls into the oven, Sarah heard

muffled voices outside the bakery. She crept closer to the door, straining to hear.

"...terrible accident at the railway," a woman's voice said, heavy with grief.

"Those poor souls," another replied. "And the Campbell girl, all alone in there. Does she know?"

Sarah's breath caught in her throat. Know what? What had happened to her parents? She pressed her ear against the door, desperate for more information, but the voices moved away, leaving her with nothing but a growing sense of dread.

Sarah's gaze darted between the bakery door and the clock on the wall, her small hands twisting the edge of her apron. The familiar ticking seemed louder than usual in the empty shop, each second stretching out like molasses. She'd lost count of how many times she'd wiped down the already spotless counter, desperate for something to do with her restless hands.

The street outside had grown quieter, but Sarah could still hear muffled voices and hurried footsteps passing by. Every now and then, someone would pause to look in through the window, their faces etched with an emotion Sarah couldn't quite name. It made her stomach twist uncomfortably.

She tried to focus on her tasks, just as her mother had taught her. There were loaves to be shaped, rolls to be scored, and the floors needed sweeping. But her mind kept wandering back to her parents. They should have been back by now.

The bell above the door remained stubbornly silent. Sarah strained to hear it, willing it to chime with every fibre of her being. But it didn't.

She moved to the window, standing on her tiptoes to peer out onto the street. The fog had lifted completely now, but the air still felt heavy, as if the entire town was holding its breath. Sarah saw Miss Havisham from next door hurrying past, her usually cheerful face drawn and pale. Their eyes met for a brief moment, and Miss Havisham quickly looked away, quickening her pace.

Sarah's frown deepened. Something was wrong, she could feel it in her bones. But what could she do? She was in charge of the bakery. She couldn't leave, not when her parents had trusted her with this responsibility.

The clock on the wall ticked past the usual time Thomas and Agatha should have returned. Sarah glanced at it with a slight frown, her light blue eyes filled with concern.

TEARS IN THE BAKERY

Sarah's fingers drummed nervously against the countertop as she peered out onto the street. The bakery's warmth felt stifling now, the smell of fresh bread cloying in her nostrils. She longed to fling open the door and run to find her parents, but her mother's words echoed in her mind.

The clock ticked relentlessly, each second stretching into an eternity. The usual bustle of Weymouth seemed muted, as if the whole town held its breath.

Sarah's gaze landed on a familiar figure approaching the bakery. Mr Thorne, the lighthouse keeper from South Point, his weathered face etched with lines of concern. He'd been a constant presence in Sarah's life, regaling her with tales of the sea and teaching her to read the weather. But today, his broad shoulders were slumped, his steps heavy.

Mr Thorne drew closer. His eyes, usually twinkling with mischief, were shadowed and grave. He paused before the bakery door, his large hand hesitating on the handle.

A cold, heavy dread settled in the pit of Sarah's stomach, spreading through her limbs like ice water. She wanted to look away, to pretend she hadn't seen him, but her eyes remained fixed on Mr Thorne's solemn face.

Mr Thorne's broad frame filled the doorway, blocking out the weak sunlight that had managed to pierce through the fog.

Sarah's legs felt leaden as she moved from behind the counter. She wanted to run, to hide in the back room among the sacks of flour and pretend this wasn't happening. But she stood her ground, chin raised as high as she could.

"Mr Thorne," she managed.

He removed his cap, twisting it in his large, calloused hands. "Sarah, lass," he began, his deep voice uncharacteristically soft. Each word seemed to pain him, as if he were forcing them past a lump in his throat.

Sarah's heart thundered, drowning out the tick of the clock and the distant murmur of voices from the street. She clenched her fists at her sides, nails digging into her palms.

Mr Thorne took a step closer, and Sarah caught the scent of sea salt and pipe tobacco that always clung to him. His presence, usually so reassuring, now felt ominous. He placed a gentle hand on her shoulder.

"There's been an accident at the railway site," Mr Thorne said, his voice gentle but filled with sorrow. "A part of one the machines came loose and crushed its way through the site…" He took in a pained breathe. "Both your parents where in its path, and…"

Sarah's world shattered as Mr Thorne's words hung heavy in the air. Her eyes, wide with disbelief, searched his face for any sign that this was all some cruel joke. But the sorrow etched in every line of his weathered features told her otherwise.

"No," she whispered, her voice trembling. "No, it can't be true!" The words tore from her throat, raw and desperate. "Mother and Father promised they'd be back. They promised!"

Sarah's legs gave way beneath her, and she would have crumpled to the floor if not for Mr Thorne's strong arms catching her. He pulled her into a tight embrace, his large frame enveloping her small one.

Sarah buried her face in Mr Thorne's rough woollen coat, her fingers clutching at the fabric as if it were a lifeline.

She felt Mr Thorne's chest heave with a deep, shuddering breath. His own grief, barely contained, mingled with hers. A warm droplet fell on her cheek, and Sarah realised it wasn't her own tear, but Mr Thorne's.

The reality of what he'd told her began to seep into her bones, turning her blood to ice. Her parents, the very centre of her world, were gone. The thought was too enormous, too terrible to comprehend fully. Sarah's mind reeled, grasping for any shred of hope, any possibility that this wasn't real.

But as Mr Thorne's arms tightened around her, as his tears fell silently into her hair, the truth became undeniable. Sarah's body shook with sobs, each one tearing through her like a physical pain. The sound of her grief, raw and primal, filled the bakery.

THE PATH FORWARD

Sarah stood in the bakery doorway, her small frame dwarfed by Mr Thorne's protective presence. A crowd of neighbours gathered outside. Their faces were etched with sympathy, eyes brimming with unshed tears for the orphaned girl.

Mrs Beatrice Wentworth who ran the tea room stepped forward, her arms outstretched. "Oh, you poor dear," she cooed, enveloping Sarah in a suffocating embrace that smelled of lavender and pity.

Sarah remained stiff, her arms hanging limply at her sides. The woman's words of comfort washed over her, meaningless as the rushing of waves against the shore. More neighbours approached, each offering condolences and promises of support, but their voices blurred together into a cacophony of well-meaning noise.

As the crowd slowly dispersed, Miss Havisham approached, her kind eyes filled with determination. "Sarah, my dear," she said softly, "I want you to know that I'll take care of the bakery. I'll run it until you're old enough to take it over yourself, if that's what you wish."

Sarah nodded mutely, a lump forming in her throat at the thought of her parents' beloved bakery continuing without them.

Mr Thorne cleared his throat, his gruff voice gentle as he addressed her. "Lass, I know it's a lot to take in, but I want you to know that you won't be alone. I'm offering to take you into my care." He paused, his weathered hand resting on her shoulder. "You'd have to move to the lighthouse with me, but it would give you a home. And I promise we'll stay in Weymouth until after your parents' funerals."

Sarah looked up at Mr Thorne, then back at Miss Havisham. Their faces were filled with genuine concern and love. She felt a flicker of warmth in the cold emptiness that had settled upon her.

Tears welled up in her eyes once more as she nodded, accepting both offers. "Thank you," she whispered, her voice barely audible. "Thank you both."

∼

As night fell, the street outside grew dark and empty, mirroring the hollow ache in Sarah's chest. She pressed her forehead against the cool glass of the window, her breath fogging the pane in rhythmic puffs.

The familiar scents of yeast and sugar still hung in the air, but now they seemed to mock her. Sarah's eyes darted to the worktable where her mother had stood just that morning, kneading dough with practiced hands. Now, it stood bare and lifeless.

"Mama," she whispered, her voice catching. "Papa."

The words hung in the air, unanswered. Sarah wrapped her arms around herself, trying to stop the trembling that had taken hold of her body. She couldn't shake the memory of her father's farewell that morning, his joyful wave as he had reappeared out of the fog to say goodbye. If only she'd hugged him, if only she'd told him one more time how much she loved him.

Sarah's gaze fell on the small clock on the mantle, its steady ticking a cruel reminder that time marched on, heedless of her world falling apart. How could everything have changed so completely in the span of a single day?

Her mind whirled with questions. Who would mend her dresses when they tore? Who would chase away the monsters under her bed? The enormity of her loss crashed over her in waves, each realisation bringing fresh tears to her eyes.

As the street lamps were lit outside, casting long shadows across the cobblestones, Sarah felt smaller than she ever had before. She longed for her mother's gentle embrace, for her father's strong arms to lift her up and tell her everything would be all right.

But they were gone, and Sarah was alone.

BENEATH SOMBRE SKIES

As the night wore on, Mr Thorne busied himself with tidying up the bakery, his movements careful and respectful. Sarah watched him through bleary eyes, grateful for his quiet presence. He set up a small bed just outside of Sarah's room, and promised he would be right there if she called out for him.

The next morning dawned grey and sombre. Miss Havisham arrived early, her kind face etched with determination. Sarah mustered what strength she could and began to show her around the bakery.

"The flour goes here," Sarah explained. She pointed to various containers and equipment, reciting the lessons her parents had taught her. "And this is how Mama always kneaded the dough."

Miss Havisham listened intently, jotting down notes and asking gentle questions. As they worked, Sarah felt a tiny spark of purpose ignite within her.

The days that followed passed in a blur of grief and preparation. Mr Thorne remained a constant presence, his gruff exterior softening as he looked after Sarah. Together, they attended to the grim necessities that followed death.

On a crisp autumn morning, Sarah stood between Mr Thorne and Miss Havisham as her parents were laid to rest. The entire town seemed to have turned out, a sea of black-clad figures paying their respects. Sarah clutched a small bouquet of wildflowers, her knuckles white with the effort of holding herself together.

As the first handfuls of earth fell upon the caskets, Sarah's knees buckle. Mr Thorne's strong arm steadied her, and Miss Havisham squeezed her hand. They were not her parents, but in that moment, Sarah was grateful not to face this alone.

A SUITCASE OF MEMORIES

Sarah stood in the middle of her room, her small suitcase packed with the few belongings she couldn't bear to leave behind. Her eyes swept across the familiar space, lingering on the faded floral wallpaper her mother had chosen and the worn rug where she'd spent countless hours playing. Everything felt different now, as if the very walls mourned the loss of her parents.

She clutched a photograph in her trembling hands, her fingers tracing the outlines of her father's kind smile and her mother's warm eyes. Thomas and Agatha Campbell gazed back at her, frozen in a moment of happiness that seemed a lifetime ago. Sarah's chest tightened, a fresh wave of grief threatening to overwhelm her.

Mr Thorne's heavy footsteps approached, and Sarah felt his presence before she saw him. She looked up at him, her eyes brimming with unshed tears.

"We'll make it through this, Miss Campbell," Mr Thorne whispered, his gruff voice soft with compassion. His words hung in the air, a promise Sarah desperately wanted to believe. She nodded, not trusting herself to speak.

With gentle guidance, Mr Thorne led her out of the room and down the stairs. Each step felt like a goodbye to the life she'd known, to the warmth and love that had filled every corner of this house.

At the bakery door, Miss Havisham waited, her eyes red-rimmed but her smile brave. "Oh, my dear girl," she said, pulling Sarah into a tight embrace. Sarah breathed in the familiar scent of flour and vanilla that clung to Miss Havisham's apron, reminding her of countless mornings spent in the bakery with her mother.

"I'll look after the bakery, Sarah," Miss Havisham promised, her voice thick with emotion. "It'll be here waiting for you when you're ready." She cupped Sarah's face in her flour-dusted hands, planting a soft kiss on her forehead.

Sarah climbed into Mr Thorne's cart, her small suitcase clutched tightly to her chest. The wooden seat felt hard and unfamiliar beneath her. Mr Thorne settled beside her, gripping the reins with practiced ease.

The cart lurched forward, its wheels groaning. Sarah's eyes burned with unshed tears as she watched her childhood home grow smaller in the distance. The bakery sign, hand-painted by her father years ago, swung gently in the breeze – a final goodbye from the life she was leaving behind.

As they trundled along the dusty road towards the lighthouse, Sarah's gaze swept across the rolling countryside beyond. It wasn't a long journey, and they probably could have walked it, but Sarah was grateful for the cart. She blinked rapidly, trying to clear her vision, but the tears kept coming.

Mr Thorne cleared his throat, stealing a glance at the small, huddled figure beside him. His heart ached for the child, wishing he knew the right words to comfort her. But comfort had never been his strong suit. He was a man of action, of steadfast reliability – not of flowery words or gentle reassurances.

"The lighthouse..." he began, his gruff voice trailing off as he realised he had no idea how to continue. He lapsed back into silence, the clip-clop of the horse's hooves filling the void between them.

Sarah barely registered Mr Thorne's attempt at conversation. Her mind was adrift in memories – her mother's laugh as they kneaded dough together, her father's strong arms lifting her high in the air. How could they be gone? The weight of her loss pressed down on her, making it hard to breathe.

Mr Thorne's eyes flicked towards Sarah again, concern etched in the deep lines of his face. He opened his mouth to speak, then closed it, the words dying on his lips. Instead, he urged the horse forward, hoping that somehow, the steady rhythm of their journey might bring a measure of peace to the grieving child beside him.

ARRIVAL AT THE LIGHTHOUSE

Sarah's eyes widened as the South Point Lighthouse came into view, its imposing form rising from the fog-shrouded coastline. The white and red stripes of the tower seemed to flicker in and out of existence as the mist swirled around it, lending an otherworldly quality to the structure.

The cart lurched to a stop. This was to be her new home, but it felt as alien as the moon. She clutched her small suitcase tighter, her knuckles turning white with the effort.

Overhead, seagulls wheeled and cried, their mournful calls mingling with the rhythmic crash of waves against the rocky shore.

Mr Thorne's weathered hands appeared before her, offering assistance. Sarah hesitated for a moment before accepting his help, her small fingers disappearing into his large, calloused palm. As she slid down from the cart, her feet hit the ground with a soft thud, and she stumbled slightly, still unsteady from the journey.

"Easy now, Miss Campbell," Mr Thorne said, his gruff voice barely audible above the din of the sea and gulls. His firm grip on her arm steadied her, which Sarah was very grateful for.

With gentle insistence, Mr Thorne guided her towards the lighthouse entrance. Sarah's legs felt leaden, each step an effort as the reality of her new situation settled heavily upon her shoulders. The lighthouse loomed ever larger as they approached, its presence both intimidating and oddly comforting in its solidity.

Sarah stepped into the lighthouse, the heavy wooden door creaking shut behind her. The sudden stillness enveloped her, a stark contrast to the tumultuous world outside. The salt air mingled with the faint aroma of oil and machinery, creating an unfamiliar yet oddly comforting atmosphere.

Her eyes darted around the room, taking in every detail. Wooden furniture, sturdy and well-worn, occupied the space. Nautical maps adorned the walls, their intricate lines and symbols a mystery to her young mind. Tools hung in perfect order on hooks and shelves, each one gleaming as if recently polished. A large well-read Bible sat on the small table beside what appeared to be Mr Thorne's reading chair.

Mr Thorne cleared his throat, drawing Sarah's attention. "This here's the main room," he said, his gruff voice softened slightly. "You'll take your meals here, and it's where we'll do most of our work."

Sarah nodded silently, her fingers still wrapped tightly around the handle of her small suitcase.

"Come along," Mr Thorne continued, gesturing towards a narrow staircase. "I'll show you to your room."

As they climbed, Sarah's free hand trailed along the cool stone wall. The lighthouse seemed to hum with a life of its own, the distant sound of waves and the occasional creak of the structure creating a constant, low murmur.

At the top of the stairs, Mr Thorne pushed open a door. "This'll be your room, Miss Campbell. It's not much, but it's warm and dry."

Sarah peered inside. A small bed sat beneath a narrow

window, a chest of drawers against one wall, and a simple writing desk in the corner. It was indeed austere, but there was a cosiness to it that Sarah couldn't quite explain.

"Thank you," she murmured.

Mr Thorne shifted uncomfortably, clearly unsure how to proceed. "Well, I'll let you get settled then. Supper's in an hour."

As he turned to leave, Sarah finally looked up at him. "Mr Thorne?"

He paused, his eyebrows raised in question.

"Thank you for taking me in," she said softly.

The lighthouse keeper only nodded, but his eyes showed the gratitude those few small words meant to him. He cleared his throat, and softly closed the door, letting Sarah settle in to her new room.

With trembling hands, Sarah placed her small suitcase on the bed. Her fingers traced the worn leather, feeling every scratch and scuff. Each mark seemed to hold a memory – her father's laughter as he'd helped her pack for a summer trip, her mother's gentle hands as she'd shown Sarah how to fold her dresses just so.

She approached the narrow window in her new room, her steps slow and hesitant. As she drew closer, the vast expanse of the waves came into view, stretching endlessly towards the horizon. The grey waters churned and roiled.

The world beyond seemed impossibly large and frighteningly empty. Sarah's eyes searched the distant waters, as if hoping to spot something familiar in the unfamiliar landscape before her.

The setting sun cast long shadows across the waves, painting the sea in hues of gold and crimson. It was beautiful, Sarah realised, but the beauty felt hollow, like a picture in a book rather than something real and alive.

As she stood there, watching the play of light on water, Sarah became acutely aware of the emptiness inside her chest. It was as if someone had scooped out everything that made her who she was, leaving behind nothing but an aching void.

But then, almost imperceptibly, Sarah felt something else creep in. A numbness began to spread through her, dulling the sharp edges of her grief. It was like a thick fog rolling in from the sea, enveloping her heart and mind in a protective shroud.

Part of Sarah wanted to fight against this numbness, to cling to the raw pain of her loss. But another part, a deeper, more instinctive part, welcomed it. This numbness was a shield, protecting her fragile heart from the full force of her sorrow.

As the last rays of sunlight disappeared below the horizon, Sarah remained at the window. The world outside had faded into shades of grey and blue, matching the muted tones of her emotions.

BETWEEN THE WAVES

Days slipped by like shadows across the lighthouse walls, each one blending into the next in a hazy blur for Sarah. The rhythmic pulse of the lighthouse lamp became the heartbeat of her new life, steady and unwavering, even as her own heart felt heavy and still.

Mr Thorne's routines dictated the flow of her days. She'd wake to the smell of strong tea and porridge, the clatter of dishes was in stark contrast to the oppressive silence that hung between them. Sarah would mechanically go through the motions of eating, her spoon scraping against the bowl in a slow, mournful rhythm.

"Care to join me up top today?" Mr Thorne would ask, his gruff voice tinged with an unfamiliar gentleness. "Got to check the lamp, make sure she's burning bright."

Sarah would nod, not meeting his eyes, and follow him up the winding stairs. The climb left her breathless, but it wasn't the exertion that made her chest feel tight. It was the memories that assaulted her with each step – memories of her father's strong hands guiding her up similar stairs, of her mother's laughter echoing in their bakery.

Mr Thorne, clearly out of his depth, tried his best to comfort her in his own way. He'd place a steaming mug of cocoa beside her as she sat staring out at the sea, or he'd recount tales of her parents from years past.

"Your father," he'd say, his voice rough with emotion, "was the bravest man I knew. Once I saw him dive into choppy waters to save a drowning child. Never hesitated, your dad."

Sarah would listen, her face a mask of indifference, even as her heart clenched painfully. She curled her fingers around the warm mug, letting the heat seep into her bones, a poor substitute for the warmth of her parents' embrace.

As days turned to weeks, Sarah retreated further into herself. She'd spend hours perched on the window seat in her small room, watching the waves crash against the rocky shore below. Mr Thorne's attempts at conversation were met with silence or, at best, monosyllabic responses.

Sarah had grown accustomed to the rhythm of Mr Thorne's movements, the way he'd pause at her door, hesitate, then continue on his way. Today, as he passed, she noticed a neatly folded blanket left by her doorway.

The gesture stirred something within her, a flicker of warmth in the cold emptiness that had become her constant companion. She hugged her knees tighter to her chest, her gaze drifting back to the churning sea beyond the window.

As the days passed, Sarah became more and more aware of Mr Thorne's quiet acts of kindness. Mr Thorne never pushed her to speak or join him, but his presence was a constant, reassuring force. Sarah would watch him from her window as he meticulously cleaned the lighthouse lens, his movements careful and practiced. Sometimes, he'd glance up at her window, a mixture of concern and hope etched on his face.

AWAKENING CURIOSITY

*S*arah sat by the lighthouse window, her small frame curled into the corner of the worn wooden seat. The waves crashed against the rocky shore.

She heard Mr Thorne's familiar footsteps approaching, the floorboards creaking under his weight. Sarah didn't turn, her gaze on the horizon where grey sea met greyer sky. She felt, rather than saw, him settle beside her on the window seat.

The silence stretched between them, broken only by the muffled roar of the waves and the occasional cry of a seabird. Mr Thorne didn't speak, didn't try to fill the quiet with empty words or forced cheer. He simply sat, a steady presence at her side, his own eyes trained on the restless waters beyond.

Sarah's fingers absently traced patterns on the cool glass, leaving fleeting imprints that faded with each breath. She could feel Mr Thorne's warmth beside her.

The minutes ticked by, marked only by the rhythmic sweep of the lighthouse beam across the turbulent sea. Sarah felt something shift within her, a tiny crack in the wall of grief she'd built around herself. Her voice, when it came, was small and weak, rough from disuse.

"Mr Thorne?" she ventured, her eyes still on the horizon. "How... how does the lighthouse work?"

She felt him turn towards her, surprise evident in the sudden intake of breath. When he spoke, his voice was gentle, careful not to shatter the fragile moment.

"Well, Miss Campbell," he began, a note of warmth creeping into his gruff tones, "it's quite a marvel, really. Would you like me to explain?"

Sarah's eyes remained fixed on the horizon, but her ears perked up at Mr Thorne's words. His voice, usually gruff and businesslike, took on a softer tone as he began to explain the workings of the lighthouse.

"You see," he said, gesturing towards the great lens at the top of the tower, "that there is the heart of our operation. It's called a Fresnel lens, invented by a clever Frenchman."

As Mr Thorne spoke, Sarah found herself drawn into the tale. She turned slightly, stealing glances as he described how the lens focused the light into a powerful beam that could be seen for miles.

"This lighthouse," he continued, a hint of pride colouring his words, "has been standing guard over these waters for nigh on thirty years now. I've been here for most of that time."

Sarah's brow furrowed. "That's a long time to be alone," she said simply.

Mr Thorne's expression softened. "Aye, it can be. But I wasn't always alone." He paused, his gaze drifting to the sea. "My Joan, she was here with me for many years. Until..."

Sarah recognised the pain in Mr Thorne's voice. She turned fully towards him now, her curiosity piqued despite the lingering fog of her own grief.

"What happened?" she asked softly.

Mr Thorne sighed, a sound as deep and melancholy as the lighthouse fog horn. "She fell ill. It was quick, too quick. One day she was here, tending her garden and laughing at the antics of the seagulls. The next..."

He trailed off, but Sarah understood. She reached out hesitantly, her small hand resting on Mr Thorne's work-worn one. For a moment, they sat in silence, united in their shared loss.

Then Mr Thorne cleared his throat. "But you know, the lighthouse taught me something important. No matter how dark the night, how fierce the storm, our light keeps shining. It guides ships to safety, just as surely as the memory of our loved ones guide us."

Sarah nodded, feeling a small spark of something she couldn't quite name. It wasn't happiness, not yet, but perhaps a glimmer of hope. She looked up at Mr Thorne, her eyes bright with curiosity.

"Could you... could you teach me more about the lighthouse?"

IN THE KEEPER'S FOOTSTEPS

Sarah watched with rapt attention as Mr Thorne's hands moved deftly across the gleaming surface of the Fresnel lens. His motions were practiced, almost reverent, as he polished the intricate glass prisms that would focus the lighthouse's beam.

"Would you like to try, Miss Campbell?" Mr Thorne asked, offering her the soft cloth.

Sarah hesitated for a moment before reaching out. The lens felt cool beneath her fingers as she mimicked Mr Thorne's movements, carefully working the cloth over the glass. She found herself lost in the repetitive motion, her mind quieting for the first time in days.

"That's it," Mr Thorne nodded approvingly. "Gentle but firm. The lens must be kept spotless to do its job properly."

Mr Thorne began involving Sarah in more of his daily tasks. She learned to check the oil levels in the lamp, to trim the wick just so, and to wind the clockwork mechanism that rotated the light. Each new skill gave her a small sense of accomplishment.

One blustery morning, Mr Thorne beckoned Sarah to join him at the small desk where he kept the lighthouse logbook.

"Time to record our observations," he explained, handing her a pencil. "What do you see out there today?"

Sarah peered out the window, taking in the choppy waves and scudding clouds. "The sea looks angry," she murmured. "And the wind's blowing hard from the southwest."

Mr Thorne nodded encouragingly. "Good eye. Now, let's write that down, nice and clear."

Sarah carefully printed her observations in the logbook, her tongue poking out slightly in concentration. As she finished, she felt a small surge of pride. Her words, there on the page, now part of the lighthouse's history.

Day by day, Sarah found herself settling into the rhythm of lighthouse life. The predictable routine of tasks became a comfort, each completed chore a small victory over the chaos of her emotions. She began to anticipate Mr Thorne's needs, fetching tools before he asked or double-checking the logbook entries without prompting.

In these shared moments of labour, the first tentative threads of connection started to form between her and Mr Thorne. They rarely spoke of personal matters, but their silences grew more comfortable, punctuated by the occasional nod of approval or quiet word of guidance.

~

Mr Thorne ladled the steaming fish stew into two earthenware bowls. The rich aroma wafted through the small kitchen, stirring memories Sarah had kept locked away. Her stomach growled, surprising her. It had been so long since she'd felt truly hungry.

Mr Thorne set the bowls on the worn wooden table and gestured for Sarah to sit. "It's not much," he said gruffly, "but it'll warm you up."

After saying grace, Sarah spooned a small bite into her

mouth. The familiar taste of flaky fish and tender vegetables flooded her senses. It was so like her mother's recipe that for a moment, Sarah felt dizzy with the force of remembering.

"It's good," she murmured. "My mother used to make something similar."

Mr Thorne's eyebrows raised slightly, but he said nothing, simply nodding for her to continue.

Sarah took another bite, savouring the comforting flavours. "She'd add a pinch of saffron when we could afford it. Said it was like capturing sunshine in the pot."

The corner of Mr Thorne's mouth twitched in what might have been a smile. He remained silent, his presence steady and patient.

Encouraged by his attentiveness, Sarah started speaking again. "My father always claimed he couldn't cook, but he made the best bread I've ever tasted. Said the secret was in how you kneaded the dough."

As she spoke, Sarah felt a warm ache spreading through her chest. The ache of loss was still there, sharp and raw, but alongside it bloomed a tender comfort in sharing these cherished memories.

"Tell me more about them," Mr Thorne said softly, his gruff voice gentler than Sarah had ever heard it.

And so, over the simple meal of fish stew, Sarah began to unfurl the stories of her parents. She spoke of her mother's laugh, her father's terrible jokes, and the way they'd dance together in the bakery kitchen when they thought she wasn't looking.

A NIGHT OF VIGILANCE

Sarah jolted awake to the sound of thunder crashing outside her window. The wind howled, rattling the glass panes as if trying to break in. She sat up, her heart racing, and peered out into the darkness. Thick fog blanketed the coast, obscuring everything beyond the lighthouse's immediate surroundings.

A sharp knock at her door made her jump.

"Miss Campbell, we need you. Come quickly." Mr Thorne's gruff voice carried a note of urgency she'd never heard before.

She scrambled out of bed, hastily pulling on her dress and shoes. When she opened the door, Mr Thorne was already halfway up the spiral staircase.

"Hurry, child. We've ships out there that need our light."

Sarah's legs burned as she raced up the steps behind him. The wind's fury grew stronger with each turn, until they reached the lantern room at the top. Mr Thorne was already at work, checking the lamp's mechanisms.

"The storm's blown in faster than expected," he explained, his eyes never leaving his task. "We need to keep the light strong and steady. Lives depend on it."

Sarah's stomach knotted with fear, but she pushed it aside. "What can I do?"

Mr Thorne glanced at her, a hint of approval in his eyes. "Check the oil levels. Make sure the reservoirs are full. We can't risk the light dimming, not tonight."

Sarah nodded, moving to the oil canisters with purpose. Her hands, once idle in her grief, now moved with growing confidence as she topped off the reservoirs. The familiar scent of the lamp oil, usually comforting, now carried a responsibility.

"Good," Mr Thorne said, his voice raised over the storm. "Now, help me with the lens. We need to ensure it's clean and rotating properly."

Together, they worked in a focused silence, broken only by Mr Thorne's occasional instructions and the relentless pounding of the waves against the rocks below. Sarah's heart raced, but she found herself oddly calm, guided by Mr Thorne's steady presence.

Sarah's eyes strained to pierce the fog. She imagined ships out there, tossed by angry waves, their crews desperately searching for the lighthouse's beam. The thought filled her with a determination she hadn't felt since before her parents' deaths.

"Mr Thorne," she called out, "I think I see a ship!"

Sarah's heart raced as she peered into the fog, her eyes straining to make out the faint outline of a ship. Mr Thorne rushed to her side, gripping the railing.

"Where, child? Show me," he urged, his voice tight with concern.

Sarah pointed, her finger trembling slightly. "There, just beyond the rocks. I can barely see it, but I'm sure it's there."

Mr Thorne squinted, then nodded grimly. "Good eye, Miss Campbell. That ship's in danger of running aground. We must keep the light strong and steady."

They sprang into action, moving with a synchronicity born of their shared purpose. Sarah checked the oil levels again, topping them off to ensure the flame burned bright. Mr Thorne adjusted the lens, his movements precise despite the urgency of the situation.

As the night wore on, Sarah's legs ached from climbing up and down the stairs, fetching supplies and tending to the light. But she pushed through her exhaustion, driven by the knowledge that lives depended on their vigilance. She could hear Mr Thorne muttering prayers to himself as he worked tirelessly, and Sarah found herself joining in with some of them.

Hours passed, the storm raging relentlessly. Just before dawn, the fog began to lift, revealing not one, but three ships that had weathered the night guided by their beacon.

Sarah let out a breath she didn't realise she'd been holding. "We did it, Mr Thorne. They're safe. Thank the Lord!"

Mr Thorne's usual stern expression softened as he looked at her. "We did indeed, Miss Campbell. You showed true grit tonight."

Warmth bloomed in Sarah's chest at his words. For the first time since losing her parents, she felt a sense of purpose, of belonging.

"I... I want to learn more," she said, surprising herself with the conviction in her voice. "About the lighthouse, the sea, everything. Will you teach me?"

Mr Thorne's eyes crinkled at the corners, the closest thing to a smile she'd seen from him. "I'd be honoured to, child. You've got the makings of a fine keeper."

As the first rays of sunlight broke through the clouds, Sarah felt something shift within her. The lighthouse, once a symbol of her loss, now represented a new beginning. She and Mr Thorne had guided ships to safety, and in doing so, had forged a bond stronger than any mere mentor and student could.

CARAMEL APPLES AND CONVERSATIONS

~~~

Sarah Campbell made her way towards the fairgrounds, her simple but neat dress swaying gently in the warm summer breeze. Her auburn hair, neatly tied back in a practical braid, caught the sunlight as she walked. A mix of excitement and mild apprehension fluttered in her with each step.

The memories of previous fairs danced at the edges of her mind, bittersweet reminders of happier times. She felt the familiar ache of loss, but today it seemed slightly less heavy. It had now been four years since her parents had so suddenly passed away, and the lively crowd surrounding her offered a welcome distraction.

As she approached, the bustling excitement of the Weymouth summer fair enveloped her. Colourful stalls were being erected, their owners calling out to one another as they arranged their wares. Vivid banners fluttered overhead, their bright hues a stark contrast to the clear blue sky.

The air was thick with the mingled scents of sweet treats and savoury delights. Sarah's nose twitched at the familiar aroma of freshly baked bread, a scent that once filled her family's bakery. For a moment, her heart clenched, but she pushed the feeling aside, determined to enjoy the day.

All around her, the sound of laughter and chatter permeated the atmosphere. Children darted between adults' legs, their excited squeals rising above the general hubbub. Townsfolk gathered in small groups, their animated conversations adding to the air of anticipation for the day's festivities.

Sarah was swept up in the energy of it all. A tight smile played at the corners of her mouth as she watched a group of young children chasing each other, their faces alight with joy. For the first time in a long while, she felt a spark of that same childlike excitement.

As she wove her way through the bustling fairgrounds, Sarah's senses were overwhelmed by the vibrant sights and sounds surrounding her. Her eyes darted from stall to stall, taking in the array of colourful trinkets and handmade crafts on display.

A group of giggling children rushed past, nearly knocking Sarah off balance. She steadied herself, her hand brushing against a table laden with intricately carved wooden figures. The vendor, an elderly man with kind eyes, nodded at her appreciatively.

"Beautiful work, isn't it?" he said, gesturing to his creations.

Sarah nodded, running her fingers over a small lighthouse figurine. For a moment, she was transported back to South Point, to Mr Thorne and the life she'd built there. She smiled softly, placing the figurine back on the table.

As she continued her stroll, the enticing aromas of festival treats wafted through the air. The aroma of freshly baked pies mingled with the sweet smell of candied almonds, making Sarah's mouth water. She paused at a stall selling steaming meat pies, remembering how her father used to treat her to one every fair day.

Just then, another enticing scent caught her attention. Sarah turned, her eyes landing on a vendor selling caramel apples. The sweet, rich aroma beckoned her. Without hesitation, she approached the stall.

"One caramel apple, please," Sarah said, fishing a coin from her pocket.

The vendor, a plump woman with rosy cheeks, handed her the treat with a warm smile. "Enjoy, dearie!"

Sarah took a bite, closing her eyes as the flavours exploded on her tongue. The crisp apple and sticky caramel brought a delighted grin to her face. For a moment, she felt like that little girl again, experiencing the simple joy of a fairground treat.

Sarah meandered through the fairgrounds, her caramel apple half-eaten in her hand. The sweet treat had lifted her spirits, and she found herself observing the bustling crowd with newfound interest. As she approached the fishmonger's stall, the pungent aroma of a fresh catch mingled with the lingering sweetness on her tongue.

A commotion near the stall caught her attention. Sarah's gaze fell upon a boy, roughly her age, who was struggling to see over the throng of people gathered around. His sun-tanned skin spoke of long hours spent outdoors, and his dark hair was tousled by the sea breeze. Sarah watched as he adjusted his cap, a look of determination etched on his face.

The boy took a step back from the crowd, his shoulders slumping slightly in defeat. There was something about his demeanour that stirred Sarah's curiosity. Despite his obvious disappointment, she noticed a quiet resilience in the set of his jaw and the way he held himself.

Sarah was drawn to this stranger. Perhaps it was the hint of shyness she detected beneath his determined exterior, or maybe it was simply the novelty of seeing someone her own age amidst the sea of adults and smaller more erratic toddlers.

Gathering her courage, Sarah took a deep breath and began

to make her way through the crowd towards the boy. Her heart beat a little faster with each step, a mix of nervousness and excitement coursing through her veins. It had been so long since she'd struck up a conversation with someone new, especially someone her own age.

As she drew closer, Sarah could see the boy more clearly. His clothes, while simple, were neat and well-kept. She noticed calluses on his hands, evidence of hard work. There was something in his eyes that spoke of a depth beyond his years, a look Sarah recognised all too well from her own reflection.

Sarah's heart skipped a beat as the boy looked up, his deep brown eyes meeting her light blue ones. She took a step forward, her hand outstretched in greeting.

"Hello, I'm Sarah Campbell," she said, her voice steady despite the flutter in her chest. "You look like you're enjoying the fair."

The boy hesitated for a moment, his eyes widening slightly in surprise. Sarah noticed a faint scar above his right eyebrow, barely visible beneath the brim of his cap. Then, as if making up his mind, he reached out and shook her hand. His grip was firm.

A sincere smile spread across his face, transforming his features. "Nice to meet you, Sarah. I'm Matthew Fletcher."

His voice was warm and rich, with a hint of shyness that Sarah found endearing. As they shook hands, she noticed the way the sunlight caught in his tousled dark hair, giving it an almost copper sheen.

Sarah felt an immediate connection with Matthew as they began to stroll through the fair together. The bustling crowds and cheerful music faded into the background as they talked, their conversation flowing with surprising ease.

"So, Matthew," Sarah ventured, her curiosity piqued, "have you lived in Weymouth long?"

Matthew nodded, his eyes scanning the horizon as if

searching for the sea. "All my life. My father raised me here, by the coast."

There was a wistful note in his voice that Sarah felt she knew herself. She waited, sensing there was more to his story.

"It's just been the two of us," Matthew continued, his voice softening. "My mother, Amelia... she died giving birth to me."

Sarah's heart clenched at his words. She reached out instinctively, her hand brushing his arm in a gesture of comfort.

Matthew gave her a small, grateful smile. "My father, Harold, he's a fisherman. He taught me everything I know about the sea and sailing."

As they passed a stall selling carved wooden boats, Matthew's eyes lit up. "Sometimes I think the sea is all we have left of her, you know? Dad says she loved watching the waves."

Sarah nodded, understanding. "I'm so sorry about your mother, Matthew. It must have been hard growing up without her."

Matthew shrugged. "It's all I've ever known. But sometimes I wonder what it would have been like..."

His voice trailed off, and Sarah felt a surge of empathy. Taking a deep breath, she decided to share her own story.

"I understand more than you might think," she said softly. "I lost both my parents four years ago. There was an accident at the railway construction site."

Matthew's eyes widened with recognition and sorrow. "I remember hearing about that. Your parents were there when it happened? I'm so sorry, Sarah."

Sarah nodded, feeling the familiar ache. "My father and mother ran the bakery in town. One day they just... didn't come home."

As they walked, Sarah almost couldn't help but start opening up about that fateful day, the words spilling out as if they'd been waiting for this moment. Matthew listened intently, his presence comforting and understanding.

The puppet show caught their attention, its vibrant curtains fluttering in the gentle breeze. Sarah was drawn to the intricate wooden figures, their painted faces animated by skilled hands behind the small stage.

"Look at that one!" Matthew pointed, his eyes twinkling with amusement as a jester puppet performed an exaggerated tumble.

Sarah laughed, the sound mingling with the delighted squeals of children around them. For a moment, she forgot her worries, lost in the simple joy of the performance.

As they moved on, the thundering of hooves drew them to the horse races. The crowd's excitement was palpable, spectators cheering and shouting encouragement to their favoured steeds. Sarah's heart raced as the horses thundered past, their powerful forms a blur of motion.

Matthew's enthusiasm was infectious. "Come on, Sarah!" he urged, pulling her closer to the fence for a better view. Their shoulders brushed as they leaned forward, caught up in the thrill of the race.

Next, they found themselves at a ring toss game. The bottles glinted in the sunlight, beckoning players to try their luck. Matthew went first, his brow furrowed in concentration as he aimed. His ring clattered against the bottles, missing by a hair's breadth.

"Your turn," he said, handing Sarah a ring with a playful grin.

Sarah took a steadying breath, focusing on the nearest bottle. She let the ring fly, watching it arc through the air. To her surprise and delight, it settled neatly around the bottle's neck.

"You did it!" Matthew cheered, his face lighting up with genuine joy for her success.

Laughing, they took turns, their competitive spirits rising with each throw.

As the afternoon wore on, the pair sampled the fair's

delectable treats. They shared a plate of honey cakes, the sweet stickiness clinging to their fingers. Matthew insisted on buying them each a bag of roasted nuts, the warm, savoury aroma making Sarah's mouth water.

DREAMS BY THE DOCKSIDE

Sarah and Matthew wandered away from the bustling fair, their feet carrying them towards the quieter docks. The sun hung low in the sky, casting a warm golden glow across the water. They found a spot on the edge of the pier, their legs dangling over the side as they settled down.

The gentle lapping of waves against the wooden pillars below filled the air, a soothing rhythm that seemed to wash away the day's excitement. Sarah breathed in deeply, the salty tang of the sea air filling her lungs. She glanced at Matthew, noticing a look of longing in his eyes.

"It's beautiful, isn't it?" Matthew said softly. "The sea, I mean. It's like it's calling to me."

Sarah nodded, understanding the pull he felt. She watched as Matthew's expression transformed, his deep brown eyes lighting up with enthusiasm.

"My father, he's the best fisherman in Weymouth," Matthew continued, his words tumbling out faster now. "The way he reads the water, knows exactly where the fish will be... it's like magic. I want to be just like him someday."

As Matthew spoke about his father's fishing skills, Sarah was drawn in by his passion. His hands moved animatedly, describing the intricate knots used in net-making and the subtle signs that indicated a good catch.

"I've been learning everything I can," Matthew said, a note of pride in his voice. "Every free moment, I'm down at the harbour, watching, helping where I can. I want to be the best fisherman Weymouth's ever seen."

Sarah listened intently, her admiration for Matthew's dedication clear in her attentive gaze. She could almost picture him out on the open water, confidently steering a boat through choppy seas.

"That's amazing, Matthew," Sarah said warmly. "I can tell how much it means to you."

Matthew turned to her, a grateful smile on his face. "What about you, Sarah? What do you dream about?"

Sarah thought about her own passion. "The lighthouse," she said, her voice filled with longing. "It's become my whole world these past few years. It's become more than just a home to me. It's feels like… it's my calling."

Matthew listened intently, his brow furrowed slightly in curiosity.

"I know it's not typical," Sarah continued, her words gaining strength. "Lighthouse keeping is a man's job, they say. But I've learned so much from Mr Thorne. The mechanics of the light, reading the weather, guiding ships safely to shore. It's all I can think about."

She paused, searching Matthew's face for any sign of judgment. Finding none, she pressed on.

"I want to be a lighthouse keeper, Matthew. I want to defy what everyone expects and show them that a woman can do this job just as well as any man."

Sarah's hands clenched in her lap, her determination evident in the set of her jaw. But then her expression softened, a flicker of uncertainty crossing her features.

"But then there's the bakery," she said, her voice dropping to almost a whisper. "It's waiting for me here in Weymouth. My parents' legacy."

Sarah's eyes misted over as she thought of the warm, flour-dusted air of the bakery, the rhythmic kneading of dough, the laughter of customers. It was a bittersweet memory.

"I don't know if I'll ever be ready to go back there," Sarah admitted, her voice tinged with uncertainty. "It's like... like stepping back into a life that doesn't exist anymore. Does that make sense?"

Sarah watched Matthew's face carefully, her heart pounding as she awaited his reaction. She'd never shared her dreams so openly before, and the vulnerability of the moment left her feeling exposed. But as she searched his eyes, she found no judgment there, only warmth and understanding.

Matthew's lips curved into a gentle smile, his eyes crinkling at the corners. "Whether it's the lighthouse or the bakery, you'll find your way, Sarah. Just like I'll navigate the sea."

His words washed over her like a soothing balm. Sarah's shoulders relaxed, a weight lifting from her chest. The sincerity in Matthew's voice touched something deep within her, a place where her doubts and fears had taken root.

"You really think so?" Sarah asked. The sea breeze ruffled her hair, carrying with it the faint scent of salt and possibilities.

Matthew nodded, his gaze steady and sure. "I do. You've got a fire in you, Sarah. I can see it when you talk about the lighthouse. It's the same way I feel about fishing."

A warmth bloomed in Sarah at his words. She'd never had someone understand her passion so completely before. It was as if Matthew could see right through to her very core.

"Thank you, Matthew," Sarah said, her voice thick with emotion. "It means more than you know to hear that."

As the sun dipped below the horizon, painting the sky in hues of orange and pink, anticipation built in the air. The fair's atmosphere had shifted, a palpable excitement rippling through the crowd as people gathered for the grand finale.

Matthew gently touched Sarah's elbow, guiding her towards a grassy knoll overlooking the fairgrounds. "We'll have the best view from up here," he said, his eyes twinkling with boyish enthusiasm.

Sarah followed, her heart light with the joy of newfound friendship. As they settled onto the grass, she noticed how the fading daylight softened Matthew's features, lending him an almost ethereal quality.

A hush fell over the crowd as the first whistle of a rocket pierced the air. Sarah held her breath, her eyes on darkening sky. Suddenly, a burst of gold exploded above them, showering the night with glittering sparks.

"Oh!" Sarah gasped, her face illuminated by the golden glow. She turned to Matthew, sharing a look of pure wonder.

More fireworks followed in quick succession, each more spectacular than the last. Brilliant reds, vibrant blues, and shimmering silvers painted the canvas of the night sky. The booms echoed in Sarah's chest.

Sarah found herself leaning closer to Matthew, their shoulders touching as they gazed upward. The colour-filled reflections danced in his eyes.

A particularly dazzling burst of green and gold elicited a chorus of "oohs" and "aahs" from the spectators. A childlike glee bubbled up inside Sarah, and she laughed out loud, the sound carrying over the explosions.

Matthew joined in her laughter, his joy as infectious as her own. In that moment, surrounded by the magic of the fireworks and the warmth of newfound friendship, Sarah felt truly alive for the first time in years.

As the grand finale approached, the sky erupted in a symphony of colour and light. Cascades of sparks rained down, creating shimmering curtains that seemed to envelop the entire world. Sarah's breath caught, overwhelmed by the beauty and the sense of possibility it ignited within her.

The final burst faded, leaving behind a trail of smoke and the lingering scent of gunpowder. In the sudden quiet, Sarah turned to Matthew, her eyes bright with excitement and something more – a spark of hope for the future.

Matthew met her gaze, his smile as warm and bright as the fireworks had been. He took her hand, his touch warm and reassuring.

"Thank you for today, Sarah," Matthew said, his voice low and earnest. "I believe in your dreams. You'll make a great lighthouse keeper someday." He continued with a small grin. "Or baker, whichever you decide."

She squeezed Matthew's hand, her smile as bright as the lighthouse beam she so loved. "And I believe in yours, Matthew," she replied. "We'll both find our way, I know we will."

The conviction in her own words surprised her. For the first time in years, Sarah felt truly certain about something. The path ahead might be unclear, but standing here with Matthew, she felt a surge of confidence that they would both achieve their dreams.

As they stood there, hands clasped, the sounds of the fair faded into the background. The salty sea breeze ruffled Sarah's hair, carrying with it the promise of adventure and new beginnings. In Matthew's steady gaze, she saw a reflection of her own determination and passion.

With a firm handshake that spoke volumes about their newfound connection, they sealed their promise to meet again. As they parted for the evening, Sarah felt lighter than she had in years, her heart buoyed by hope and the warmth of friendship.

EVENING REFLECTIONS

Sarah trudged up the winding path to South Point Lighthouse, her feet aching from a day of wandering the fair. The familiar silhouette of the lighthouse loomed against the inky night sky, its powerful beam sweeping across the dark waters.

Mr Thorne stood by the door, his weathered face illuminated by the soft glow of a lantern. His eyes crinkled with affection as he watched Sarah's approach.

"There you are, lass," he called out, his gruff voice carrying on the sea breeze. "How was your day at the fair?"

Sarah quickened her pace, eager to share her experiences. As she reached the doorway, she found herself practically bursting with enthusiasm.

"Oh, Mr Thorne, it was wonderful!" she exclaimed, her eyes shining. "The fair was so alive with colour and music. And I made a new friend!"

Mr Thorne's eyebrows rose, a subtle smile tugging at the corners of his mouth. "Did you now? Well, come inside and tell me all about it."

They settled into the cosy main room, the familiar scents of oil and salt air wrapping around them. Sarah perched on the edge of her chair, hands animated as she recounted her adventures.

"His name is Matthew Fletcher," she began, her words tumbling out in a rush. "He lost his mother too, so he understands. We explored the fair together – oh, Mr Thorne, you should have seen the puppet show! And the horse races were so thrilling!"

Mr Thorne listened intently, his hands clasped in his lap. The subtle smile never left his face as he watched Sarah's excitement unfold.

"We talked about our dreams," Sarah continued, her voice softening. "Matthew wants to be a fisherman like his father. And I told him about wanting to be a lighthouse keeper." She paused, her eyes meeting Mr Thorne's. "He believes in me, Mr Thorne. He said I'd make a great lighthouse keeper someday."

Mr Thorne nodded, his eyes twinkling. "Sounds like a fine lad, this Matthew. I'm glad you've found a friend, Sarah. It does my heart good to see you smiling again."

∼

Sarah lay in her small bed, the familiar creaks and groans of the lighthouse mingling with the distant crash of waves against the rocky shore. Her mind buzzed with the day's events, replaying each moment like a treasured picture book.

The warmth of Matthew's newfound friendship lingered, a comforting presence in the quiet darkness. She thought of his easy smile, the way his eyes lit up when he spoke about the sea. It reminded her of her mother's passion for baking, how her hands would lovingly shape each loaf.

Sarah's heart ached at the memory, but for the first time since the accident, it wasn't an overwhelming pain. Instead, it felt like a bittersweet reminder of the love that had shaped her.

She turned her gaze to the window, where the lighthouse's beam swept across the inky blackness. Mr Thorne's patient teachings came to mind – the intricate workings of the Fresnel lens, the importance of keeping the light burning bright. His gruff kindness had become a steady anchor in her new life.

As Sarah's eyelids grew heavy, a calm settled over her. The fair had awakened something within her – a spark of joy she thought lost forever. Matthew's belief in her dream of becoming a lighthouse keeper echoed in her mind, bolstering her own conviction.

The rhythmic sweep of the beam lulled her towards sleep. Sarah's last conscious thoughts were of lighthouses dotting a misty coastline, their beacons cutting through fog and darkness. In her mind's eye, she stood atop one such lighthouse, Matthew by her side, both of them gazing out at the vast, open sea.

A small smile played on Sarah's lips as she drifted off, the future no longer seeming quite so daunting. With Matthew's friendship and Mr Thorne's guidance, she felt ready to face whatever challenges lay ahead.

PART II
SHADOWS ON THE SHORE

1865-1866

THE WINDS OF CHANGE

Sarah stood atop the lighthouse, her keen eyes sweeping across the transformed landscape of Weymouth. It had changed so much in just six years. The newly completed railway cut a sleek path through the town, its iron tracks gleaming in the afternoon sun. She marvelled at how quickly things had changed in the years since that fateful summer fair.

The distant whistle of an approaching locomotive pierced the air, mingling with the familiar roar of the ocean. Sarah closed her eyes for a moment, letting the sounds wash over her. It was a strange symphony – the rhythmic chug of engines blending with the timeless crash of waves against the shore. Progress and tradition, woven together in an ever-changing melody.

As she descended the lighthouse stairs, her mind drifted to the bustling streets below. Weymouth was barely recognisable from the quiet town of her childhood. Now, it seemed to burst at the seams with activity. Every day brought new faces – tourists with their wide-eyed wonder, traders laden with exotic goods, and workers seeking their fortunes in this booming seaside haven. Sarah was thankful to God for all he had given her, both new and old.

Mr Thorne's gruff voice called out as she reached the bottom of the stairs. "Sarah! Mind helping me with these supplies? Seems half of London's decided to vacation here this week."

She hurried to assist, grasping one end of a heavy crate. As they manoeuvred it into the storage room, Sarah couldn't help but smile at the old lighthouse keeper's exasperation. "It's not so bad, is it?" she asked. "All this new life in town?"

Mr Thorne harrumphed, but there was a twinkle in his eye. "Suppose not. Though I'll never get used to all that racket from those blasted trains."

Sarah laughed, her gaze drawn to the window. From here, she could just about make out the main street, teeming with activity. Weymouth had also grown in size as well as commerce. Shops that had once struggled now overflowed with customers. New businesses seemed to spring up overnight, their freshly painted signs promising all manner of goods and services.

Sarah felt a mix of excitement and apprehension as she watched the changes unfolding in Weymouth. The town she'd known as a child was transforming before her eyes, growing and stretching like a living thing.

Sarah was drawn back to the top of the lighthouse once she had finished assisting Mr Thorne.

Her gaze drifted to the harbour, where fishing boats now jostled for space alongside sleek pleasure craft. She thought of Matthew, out there somewhere on his father's boat, and wondered if he felt the same conflicting emotions about Weymouth's rapid growth.

The Esplanade, once a quiet stretch of shoreline, now teemed with life. Fashionable ladies twirled parasols as they promenaded arm-in-arm with gentlemen in smart suits. Children squealed with delight as they splashed in the waves or built elaborate sandcastles. The sounds of laughter and chatter carried on the wind, a stark contrast to the solitude Sarah had grown accustomed to.

As she descended the lighthouse steps, Sarah's mind whirled with possibilities. The influx of visitors meant more ships to guide safely to shore, more lives depending on the steady beam of light she and Mr Thorne maintained. It was a weighty responsibility, but one that filled her with pride.

Yet beneath her excitement lurked a kernel of worry. Would this new, bustling Weymouth still have a place for a girl who'd grown up in the quiet shadows of tragedy? Could she navigate this changed landscape as deftly as she navigated the treacherous waters of the coast?

Sarah leaned against the lighthouse railing, her auburn hair whipping in the salty breeze as she watched a familiar figure trudging up the rocky path. A smile tugged at her lips as Matthew's broad-shouldered form came into view, his gait steady and sure-footed from years of balancing on fishing boats.

"Ahoy there, lighthouse keeper!" Matthew called out, his now deep voice carrying on the wind.

Sarah's heart warmed towards her friend. "And what news do you bring from the briny deep, Master Fletcher?" she called back, falling easily into their playful banter.

As Matthew reached the top, Sarah couldn't help but notice how the years had changed him. Gone was the gangly boy she'd met at the fair; in his place stood a man weathered by the sea, his skin tanned and his hands calloused from years of working the nets.

"You won't believe the catch we had today," Matthew said, his deep brown eyes sparkling with excitement. "Found a new spot just beyond the bay. The cod were practically jumping into the boat!"

Sarah listened intently as Matthew regaled her with tales of his latest fishing expedition. His animated gestures and vivid descriptions painted a picture of life on the water that both fascinated and comforted her. Though their paths had diverged – Sarah tending the lighthouse while Matthew followed in his father's footsteps – their friendship remained a steadfast anchor.

"Sounds like quite the adventure," Sarah said, a hint of wistfulness in her voice. "Sometimes I envy you, out there on the open sea."

Matthew's expression softened. "Aye, but we couldn't do it without you keeping that light burning bright. You're our guiding star, Sarah."

A comfortable silence fell between them, broken only by the cry of gulls and the distant crash of waves.

"What do you say we go for a walk?" Matthew suggested suddenly. "I've got an hour before I need to head back."

Sarah nodded eagerly, grateful for the chance to stretch her legs and explore. Together, they made their way down the lighthouse path and onto the rocky shoreline below. Matthew's strong hand steadied her as they navigated the uneven terrain, a gesture that sent a flutter through her chest.

As they picked their way along the coast, a sense of peace washed over Sarah. Here, with the familiar rhythm of the tide and Matthew's solid presence beside her, she could forget about the rapid changes overtaking Weymouth. For now, it was just the two of them, the sea, and the endless horizon stretching out before them.

BETWEEN WORLDS

Sarah's boots crunched against the pebbles as she walked alongside Matthew. The salty air whipped tendrils of her hair free from her braid, and she tucked them behind her ear with a practiced gesture.

As they rounded a bend in the shoreline, the full expanse of Weymouth's harbour came into view. Sarah paused, her gaze drawn to the forest of masts and the bustle of activity along the waterfront.

"Sometimes I wonder if they would have been proud of all this change," she mused, her voice steady yet tinged with sadness.

Matthew halted beside her, his presence solid and reassuring. His calloused hand found hers, giving it a gentle squeeze. "They would be proud of you, Sarah. You've come so far."

Sarah turned to face him, searching his sun-weathered features. The sincerity in his eyes chased away some of the melancholy that had settled over her.

"It's just..." she began, struggling to put her conflicted feelings into words. "The bakery, the lighthouse, this new Weymouth – sometimes it feels like I'm caught between different worlds."

Matthew nodded, understanding etched in the furrow of his brow. "Change isn't easy," he said softly. "But you've faced it head-on, Sarah. You've made a place for yourself here, just as your parents did in their time."

Sarah's gaze drifted back to the harbour, taking in the mix of fishing boats and pleasure craft. "I suppose you're right," she admitted. "It's just hard to shake the feeling that I'm somehow letting them down by not returning to the bakery."

"Your parents wanted you to find your own path," Matthew reminded her gently. "And look at what you've accomplished. You're keeping ships safe, saving lives. That's something to be proud of."

Sarah watched the ships glide into the harbour, their sails catching the late afternoon light. The familiar creaking of wood and the calls of seagulls filled the air. She breathed in deeply, savouring the salty tang, as she sat down on a weathered wooden bench that had been there for as long as she could remember. At least some things seemed constant and never-changing.

Matthew sat beside her on the bench, his leg bouncing with barely contained excitement. "You know, Sarah," he began, his eyes sparkling with enthusiasm, "I've been thinking about expanding my fishing operation."

Sarah turned to face him, intrigued. "Oh? What did you have in mind?"

Matthew leaned forward, his voice eager. "Well, I've been saving up, and I reckon I could afford a larger boat. One that could handle longer trips, maybe even venture out to some of the deeper fishing grounds."

Sarah nodded, her mind already racing with the possibilities. "That could be quite profitable," she mused. "But it would also mean longer times away from port."

"Exactly," Matthew agreed. "It's a bit daunting, but I think it's the right move. The demand for fish in Weymouth is growing every day with all these new tourists."

Sarah smiled, proud of her friend's ambition. "You've always had a good head for business, Matthew. I think you're onto something here."

Matthew's grin widened at her encouragement. "I've been studying the tides and currents," he continued, pulling out a small, leather-bound notebook from his pocket. "Been keeping track of where the best catches are coming from."

Sarah leaned in, examining the neat rows of figures and observations. "This is impressive, Matthew. Have you thought about how you'll crew a larger vessel?"

Matthew nodded eagerly. "I've got a few lads in mind. Good, steady workers who know their way around a boat."

"And what about the market?" Sarah asked, her practical side coming to the fore. "Have you spoken with any of the local fishmongers about taking on larger orders?"

Matthew's expression turned sheepish. "Well, not yet. I wanted to get the boat first."

Sarah laid a gentle hand on his arm. "Why don't we go talk to Mr Browning at the market tomorrow? He's always complaining about not having enough fresh fish to meet demand. I bet he'd be interested in a steady supply."

Matthew's eyes lit up. "That's brilliant, Sarah! I knew I could count on you to see the angles I'd missed."

It felt good to be useful, to help Matthew chase his dreams. "That's what friends are for," Sarah said softly. "We look out for each other."

HEARTS IN HARMONY

A group of visitors gathered at the base of the lighthouse, their excited chatter carried up to her on the wind. Sarah smiled, remembering her initial surprise when people had first started showing interest in touring the lighthouse.

"Sarah!" Mr Thorne's gruff voice called from below. "The new group's here. Are you ready?"

"Coming, Mr Thorne!" she replied, giving the sea one last glance before descending the spiral staircase.

She found Mr Thorne at the entrance, a small crowd of eager faces peering past him into the lighthouse's interior. She noticed the slight tension in his shoulders, a remnant of his initial reluctance to open their sanctuary to outsiders.

"Good afternoon, everyone," Sarah greeted the group warmly. "Welcome to South Point Lighthouse. I'm Sarah, and I'll be your guide today."

As she led the group inside, explaining the history and function of the lighthouse, Sarah felt a familiar thrill. She loved sharing her knowledge, seeing the wonder in people's eyes as they learned about the crucial role lighthouses played in maritime safety.

"And this," Sarah said, gesturing to the magnificent Fresnel lens, "is the heart of our operation. It's what allows our light to be seen for miles out to sea."

A young boy raised his hand, eyes wide with curiosity. "How does it work, Miss?"

Sarah's face lit up at the question. She launched into an explanation of the lens's intricate design, her passion evident in every word. Mr Thorne, observing from the corner, couldn't help but smile at her enthusiasm.

As the tour progressed, Sarah's confidence grew. She fielded questions with ease, her deep understanding of lighthouse operations shining through. The visitors hung on her every word, clearly impressed by her knowledge and dedication.

∽

THE MARKETPLACE BUSTLED as Sarah stood with her basket laden with fresh produce. She smiled, greeting Mrs Hawkins at her vegetable stall.

"Good morning, Mrs Hawkins! Those carrots look splendid today."

"Mornin', Sarah love. Take your pick, they're fresh from the garden."

As Sarah selected her vegetables, she overheard a group of newcomers discussing the upcoming summer fete. Their excitement was palpable, and Sarah was drawn into their conversation.

"Excuse me," she said, turning to the group. "I couldn't help but overhear. Are you planning to attend the fete?"

A woman with a warm smile replied, "Oh yes! We've heard so much about it. Do you know where we can find more information?"

Sarah's eyes lit up. "Actually, I'm helping to organise it this year. Would you like me to show you around?"

As she guided the newcomers through the marketplace, Sarah pointed out local attractions and shared tidbits about Weymouth's history. The town that had once been a source of such pain was now brimming with life and possibility.

Later that afternoon, at the town hall, Sarah was surrounded by a flurry of activity as volunteers prepared for the fete. She worked alongside familiar faces and new friends, hanging banners and arranging stalls.

"Sarah, dear," Miss Havisham called from across the room. "Could you help me with these flowers?"

As Sarah arranged bouquets with her old neighbour, memories of doing the same with her mother surfaced. They were happy memories, and the sting of pain was lessening with each year.

She turned back to Miss Havisham, a gentle smile on her face. "You know, I think my mother would have loved these flowers. She always said a touch of colour could brighten even the darkest day."

Miss Havisham squeezed her hand, understanding in her eyes. "She was right, my dear. And look at you now, bringing that brightness to our whole town."

THE STRETCH OF TRADITION

Sarah noticed the tension in the air as she walked through the marketplace. The once-familiar faces of long-time residents now bore frowns and furrowed brows. She overheard snippets of conversation, laced with discontent.

"Too many strangers about," Mrs Wentworth muttered to her friend. "Can't even recognise half the faces I see nowadays."

Sarah's heart sank. She understood the discomfort of change, but she also saw the benefits the transformation had brought to Weymouth. As she passed by The Broken Compass, one of the seedier pubs, she heard raised voices.

"You can't just change everything overnight!" Margery "Mags" Black shouted at a well-dressed gentleman. "This town has traditions, you know!"

Sarah stepped forward, her voice calm but firm. "Mrs Black, is everything all right?"

The bar owner turned, her face red with anger. "This fellow here wants to buy out half the street and turn it into some fancy promenade!"

Sarah turned to the gentleman, who looked flustered. "Sir,

perhaps we could discuss this over tea? I'm sure there's a way to honour our town's history while embracing progress."

Her words seemed to diffuse the tension. Both of them nodded, albeit reluctantly.

As she walked away, Sarah felt the weight of responsibility on her shoulders. She had become a bridge between the old and the new, a role she never expected to fill.

That evening, as she helped Mr Thorne with the lighthouse duties, Sarah shared her concerns.

"It's like the town is split in two," she sighed. "Those who welcome the changes and those who resist them."

Mr Thorne nodded sagely. "Change is never easy, Sarah. But it's necessary. Like the tides, it comes whether we want it or not."

"But how do we help everyone see that?" Sarah asked, her brow furrowed.

"By doing exactly what you're doing," Mr Thorne replied. "Listening, understanding, and finding common ground."

Later, as she walked along the shore with Matthew, Sarah finally could voice her fears.

"I'm worried, Matthew. What if these tensions tear the town apart?"

Matthew squeezed her hand reassuringly. "We won't let that happen, Sarah. This town is our home. We'll find a way to bring everyone together."

AGAINST THE ROCKS

Sarah's keen eyes were fixed looking through the powerful telescope. The sun had barely risen, painting the sky in hues of pink and gold. She adjusted the lens, focusing on a distant speck on the horizon. As the image sharpened, the merchant ship 'Lady Isabel' came into view, its elegant form cutting through the water with grace and purpose.

The vessel's tall masts reached towards the cloudless sky, full sails billowing in the gentle breeze. Sarah marvelled at the sight, admiring the ship's sleek lines and the way it seemed to glide effortlessly across the waves.

With practiced movements, Sarah began to monitor the ship's course. She jotted down observations in the logbook, her neat handwriting filling the page with details of 'Lady Isabel's' position and speed. The ship was following a well-charted route, one that Sarah had seen countless vessels take before.

The weather couldn't have been more perfect for sailing. A clear blue sky stretched as far as the eye could see, unmarred by even the faintest wisp of cloud. The sea was calm, its surface broken only by gentle swells that posed no threat to 'Lady Isabel's' journey.

Sarah's brow furrowed as she continued to observe 'Lady Isabel' through the telescope. Something wasn't right. The ship's course had shifted ever so slightly, veering closer to the treacherous rocks that lined the coast near South Point. She blinked hard, certain her eyes were playing tricks on her.

But they weren't.

'Lady Isabel' was heading straight for danger.

Sarah's heart began to race. She wanted to shout, to warn them somehow, but knew her voice could never carry that far. She watched, helpless, as the magnificent vessel drew closer and closer to the jagged rocks.

Then it happened.

The sickening sound of wood meeting stone filled the air. Sarah gasped as she witnessed 'Lady Isabel' lurch violently, its hull scraping against the unforgiving rocks. The telescope shook in her trembling hands, but she couldn't tear her eyes away from the unfolding disaster.

The ship's elegant form, which had cut so gracefully through the water mere moments ago, now tilted at a horrifying angle. Sarah could hear the distant, panicked shouts of the crew even from her position in the lighthouse. Men scrambled across the deck, their movements frantic and desperate.

Sarah's mind raced. How could this be happening? The weather was perfect, the sea calm, and the lighthouse beam had been shining brightly all night. There was no reason for 'Lady Isabel' to have strayed so far off course.

As she watched, the ship began to take on water at an alarming rate. Its stern dipped lower into the sea, waves now lapping at the deck. The crew's shouts grew more urgent, their fear palpable even from a distance.

Sarah's heart pounded. She had to do something, had to help somehow.

She tore down the lighthouse stairs, her footsteps echoing

off the stone walls. "Mr Thorne!" she called out, her voice urgent and breathless. "'Lady Isabel' has struck the rocks!"

Mr Thorne appeared at the bottom of the staircase, concern etched in every line. "What's happened, lass?"

Sarah quickly relayed what she'd witnessed, her words tumbling out in a rush. Mr Thorne's expression grew grave as he listened, his mind already formulating a plan.

"Right," he said, his voice steady and commanding. "We've no time to lose. Sarah, run to the harbour and alert the fishermen. I'll sound the alarm bell."

Sarah nodded, determination setting her jaw. She burst out of the lighthouse, her legs carrying her swiftly towards the town. The cool morning air whipped at her face as she ran, her lungs burning with exertion.

As she reached the harbour, Sarah's voice rang out across the water. "Help! 'Lady Isabel' is wrecked on the rocks! We need every able hand!"

Her cries were met with immediate action. Fishermen emerged from their boats and homes, faces set with grim resolve. Among them, Sarah spotted Matthew Fletcher, his dark hair tousled by the sea breeze.

"Matthew!" she called out. "We need your help!"

He nodded, already moving to prepare his father's boat. "I'm with you, Sarah," he shouted back, his voice carrying over the growing commotion.

The harbour erupted into a flurry of activity. Men rushed to launch rowboats, their movements quick and purposeful. Women gathered blankets and bandages, preparing for the rescued crew. The community, so often divided in recent times, now united in the face of a crisis.

Sarah found herself in the thick of it all, her lighthouse training proving invaluable. She helped organise the rescue efforts, her calm voice cutting through the chaos. "We'll need ropes," she instructed a group of men. "And lanterns, in case a fog rolls in."

As the first boats pushed off from the shore, Sarah felt a hand on her shoulder. She turned to see Mr Thorne, his face etched with pride. "Well done, lass," he said. "Now, let's get out there and bring those men home."

Without hesitation, Sarah climbed into one of the waiting boats. Matthew was already at the oars, his strong arms propelling them towards the open sea. As they cut through the waves, Sarah's eyes remained on the horizon, where the stricken 'Lady Isabel' awaited their aid.

'Lady Isabel', once a proud merchant vessel, now lay broken and battered against the merciless rocks. Its masts leaned at sickening angles. The ship listed dangerously to one side, its deck awash with seawater that sloshed violently with each passing wave.

The air was thick with the acrid smell of saltwater and splintered wood. Sarah's nose wrinkled at the pungent odour. Crates and barrels bobbed in the choppy waters, the ship's cargo scattered like children's toys in a bathtub. But it wasn't the lost goods that made Sarah's breath catch in her throat – it was the crew.

Men thrashed in the water, their cries of distress cutting through the air. Some clung desperately to floating debris, while others struggled to keep their heads above the relentless waves. Their shouts mingled with the urgent calls of the rescuers, creating a cacophony of fear and determination.

"There!" Sarah pointed, her voice steady despite the chaos around her. "To the starboard side!"

Matthew steered their boat towards a group of sailors clinging to a broken piece of mast. As they drew near, Sarah leaned over the side, her hands outstretched.

"Here," she called, her voice clear and strong. "Take my hand!"

A sailor, his face pale with fear and exhaustion, reached out. Sarah grasped his wrist, her grip firm and sure. With a strength born of countless hours working in the lighthouse, she hauled him towards the boat. Matthew steadied the craft as Sarah guided the man to safety.

"Thank you, miss," the sailor gasped, collapsing onto the floor of the rowboat.

But Sarah had no time for thanks. Her eyes were already searching for the next soul in need of rescue. She spotted a young cabin boy, barely treading water amidst the debris.

"Row, Matthew!" she urged, her voice tight with urgency.

As they approached, Sarah reached out once more. Her hands found the boy's slippery arm. With a grunt of effort, she pulled him from the sea's grasp, guiding him into the relative safety of their small craft.

AMIDST THE WRECKAGE

*S*arah's feet sank into the wet sand as she helped guide the rescued sailors onto the shore. The beach, usually a place of leisurely strolls and children's laughter, had transformed into a scene of organised chaos. Debris from 'Lady Isabel' littered the shoreline.

The air was thick with the smell of brine and fear. Sarah moved swiftly among the crowd, her arms laden with woollen blankets. She draped them over shivering sailors, her touch gentle yet purposeful. Her eyes scanned the beach, taking in the sight of limping men and concerned townsfolk who had gathered to help.

"Here," she said, pressing a steaming mug of tea into the hands of a sailor with salt-crusted hair. "This'll warm you up."

The man nodded gratefully, his hands trembling as he took the cup. Sarah's gaze swept over him, checking for any visible injuries. Satisfied he was relatively unharmed, she moved on to the next person in need.

Her heart skipped a beat when she spotted Matthew. He was hunched over, favouring his left side. A nasty gash ran along his forearm, an angry red against his tanned skin.

"Matthew!" Sarah rushed to his side, her voice laced with concern. "What happened?"

He looked up, a wry smile tugging at his lips despite the pain evident in his eyes. "Got tangled in some ropes while pulling a fellow out. It's nothing, Sarah."

But Sarah knew better. She guided Matthew to sit on an overturned crate, her touch firm but gentle. "Let me see to that," she insisted, already reaching for the medical supplies Miss Havisham had brought from town.

As Sarah cleaned Matthew's wound, her movements were steady and sure. She worked in silence, her brow furrowed in concentration. Matthew watched her, his admiration evident in his gaze.

"There," Sarah said, tying off the bandage. "That should hold."

She was about to stand when a pained groan caught her attention. A sailor nearby was cradling his arm, his face contorted in agony. Without hesitation, Sarah moved to his side.

"Let me see," she said softly, her voice calm and reassuring. The sailor looked up, his eyes wide with fear and pain. Gently, Sarah examined his arm, noting the dark bruising and swelling.

"It's not broken," she assured him, her hand resting lightly on his shoulder. "But it's a nasty bruise. We'll get you something for the pain soon."

The sailor nodded, visibly relaxing under Sarah's care. She stayed with him, her presence a balm in the midst of the chaos. Her words were soft, yet carried a strength that seemed to anchor those around her.

Sarah's eyes scanned the chaotic scene on the beach, her gaze moving from one weary face to another. Amidst the crowd of shivering sailors and concerned townsfolk, she spotted a solitary figure. Captain William Everett sat apart from the others, his shoulders slumped and his eyes fixed on some distant point beyond the tumultuous sea.

The weight of command seemed to press down upon him, etching deep lines into his face. His salt-and-pepper hair was dishevelled, and his once-pristine uniform hung in tatters. A long scar across his left cheek stood out starkly against his pale skin. Defeat hung heavy in the air around him.

Sarah felt a pang of sympathy for the man. She'd heard tales of Captain Everett's skill and bravery from the sailors who frequented Weymouth's harbour. To see such a respected mariner brought low by the cruel whims of the sea stirred something within her.

Without hesitation, Sarah grabbed a flask of water and made her way towards the captain. As she drew near, she could see the haunted look in his eyes.

"Captain Everett?" Sarah's voice was soft but steady as she approached. She held out the flask, a simple offering of comfort. "I thought you might need this."

The captain's gaze slowly shifted from the horizon to Sarah's face. For a moment, he seemed to look right through her, lost in the depths of his own thoughts. Then, with visible effort, he focused on her outstretched hand.

"Thank you, miss," he murmured, his voice hoarse. He accepted the flask with trembling fingers but made no move to drink.

Sarah settled herself on the sand beside him, close enough to offer support but not so near as to intrude. She said nothing, simply providing a steady presence as the captain wrestled with his thoughts.

Sarah's attention was drawn to a small gathering of sailors huddled near the water's edge. The wind carried fragments of their hushed conversation to her ears, and she found herself straining to catch every word.

"It doesn't make sense in clear weather," one of the sailors muttered, his voice filled with confusion.

Sarah's brow furrowed as she pretended to busy herself with

sorting through medical supplies. Her hands moved mechanically, but her focus was entirely on the group of men.

Another sailor chimed in, his tone laced with suspicion. "Couldn't have been an accident. Not with conditions like that."

The captain's voice trembled slightly as he spoke, a stark contrast to the commanding presence Sarah had always associated with him. "How could such a catastrophe happen under ideal conditions?" His gaze was distant, troubled, as if searching the horizon for answers that eluded him.

Sarah had seen the sea in all its moods from her perch in the lighthouse, knew its patterns and temperaments. The idea that something beyond nature's whims might be at play sent a chill down her spine.

She risked a glance at Captain Everett. His shoulders were slumped. His crew looked to him for answers, but it was clear he had none to give.

The Captain's fingers tightened around the flask she'd given him, his knuckles turning white with the force of his grip.

After a long moment, Captain Everett turned to her, his face etched with worry. His voice was low, almost a whisper, as if he feared being overheard.

"Miss, I... I can't make sense of it," he began, his eyes searching Sarah's face as if hoping to find answers there. "We were sailing smooth, the weather was clear as crystal. Then, in the blink of an eye..."

He trailed off, shaking his head in disbelief. Sarah leaned in slightly.

"The ship, she just... veered. Like she had a mind of her own," Captain Everett continued, his voice gaining strength as he spoke. "I've been at sea for decades, and never have I seen anything like it. One moment we were on course, the next..."

His eyes darted to the wreckage strewn across the beach, a visible shudder running through his body. "We were headed straight for the rocks. No warning, no time to correct. It was as if some unseen force had taken hold of the rudder."

Sarah's brow furrowed as she listened, her mind racing to make sense of the captain's account. She'd seen countless ships navigate these waters from her vantage point at the lighthouse, knew the currents and tides like the back of her hand. What the captain described seemed impossible, yet the evidence of the disaster lay scattered around them.

"I've weathered storms that would make the bravest sailor quake," Captain Everett muttered, a mixture of frustration and fear in his eyes. "But this? This defies explanation. It's as if the sea itself turned against us."

The clear weather and full operation of the lighthouse should have ensured safe passage for 'Lady Isabel'. Yet, here they were, surrounded by the wreckage of a ship that by all rights should have sailed smoothly past South Point Lighthouse.

The rumours among the crew echoed in her ears, their hushed tones carrying a weight of suspicion that seemed to hang in the salty air. Sarah glanced at the gathered sailors, noting their furtive glances and tense postures. Something more than just a simple accident had occurred here, something that had shaken these seasoned mariners to their core.

Sarah's fingers curled into fists at her sides, her nails digging into her palms. The implications were staggering. If the wreck wasn't an accident, if something more nefarious was at play...

Sarah's ears pricked at a young sailor's hushed words, barely audible above the crash of waves and the commotion on the beach. Her eyes darted to the lad, taking in his nervous demeanour, the way his fingers twisted anxiously in the hem of his salt-stained shirt.

"Maybe... maybe someone meddled with our course," he muttered, his voice trembling.

The words hung in the air, heavy as storm clouds. Before

Sarah could process the thought, Captain Everett's voice cut through the tension like a knife.

"Enough of that talk, boy!" he barked, his face stern. "We'll have none of that speculation here."

But Sarah caught the flicker of doubt that passed across the captain's eyes. It was there for just a moment, a shadow of uncertainty that belied his firm words.

The young sailor ducked his head, properly chastised, but the seed of suspicion had been planted. Sarah's gaze swept over the gathered crew, noting the uneasy glances exchanged, the hushed whispers that seemed to carry more weight than mere accident talk.

As she watched, a familiar spark ignited within her. It was the same feeling she got when she spotted a ship in distress from the lighthouse, that urgent need to act, to help, to set things right. But this time, it wasn't about guiding ships to safety. This was about uncovering a truth that someone seemed desperate to keep hidden.

Resolve hardened within Sarah. The mystery of 'Lady Isabel's' wreck tugged at her, demanding answers. Sarah knew she couldn't let this go, not when so many lives had been put at risk, not when the shadow of sabotage loomed so ominously over the wreckage strewn across the beach.

With a deep breath, Sarah straightened her shoulders. She may not have known exactly how, but she was determined to get to the bottom of this. The truth was out there, hidden beneath the waves or lurking in the whispers of the crew, and Sarah Campbell was going to find it.

PACT OF THE TRIO

~~~

Sarah's feet crunched on the gravel path leading up to the lighthouse, her mind whirling like the beacon above. Matthew kept pace beside her, his usual easy gait replaced by a tense stride that matched her own urgency. His arm was bandaged and in a sling.

They found Mr Thorne in the lantern room. He turned at their approach, his bushy eyebrows rising at the sight of their grave expressions.

"Mr Thorne," Sarah began, her voice steadier than she felt, "something's not right about the 'Lady Isabel' wreck."

The old lighthouse keeper's eyes narrowed, the stormy grey of his irises seeming to churn like the sea itself. He set down his polishing cloth, giving them his full attention.

Sarah recounted what she'd overheard on the beach, her words tumbling out in a rush. She described Captain Everett's bewilderment, the impossible veering of the ship, and the hushed whispers of sabotage among the crew. Matthew chimed in, adding details she'd missed and confirming the strange atmosphere that had permeated the rescue efforts.

As they spoke, Mr Thorne's expression grew increasingly

grave. His gnarled fingers stroked his beard. He didn't interrupt, save for the occasional grunt or nod, his eyes never leaving their faces as they laid out the disturbing puzzle pieces.

When they finished, silence fell over the lantern room. The only sound was the faint whistle of wind around the lighthouse and the gentle lapping of waves far below. Mr Thorne's gaze drifted to the vast expanse of sea visible through the glass.

"This is a serious matter," Mr Thorne said, his voice low and gravelly. "If there's truth to these whispers, it could mean more than just one ship at risk."

Matthew nodded, wincing slightly as the movement jostled his injured arm. "But who would want to sabotage a merchant ship? And why?"

Sarah's mind whirled with possibilities, each more unsettling than the last. She thought of the bustling harbour, the lifeblood of Weymouth, and how vulnerable it suddenly seemed.

Mr Thorne straightened, his posture rigid. "I'll reach out to Captain Holloway at the maritime office first thing tomorrow. He's got connections with the coastguard as well. I can also mention it to Jonathan Leighton. He's retired now, but was in the navy for more years than you've seen. We need to tread carefully, but swiftly."

"And what can we do?" Sarah asked, leaning forward, eager to help.

The old lighthouse keeper's eyes softened as he looked at her. "Keep your eyes and ears open, lass. You've got a sharp mind and a way with people. Folks trust you. They might let slip things they'd never tell an old codger like me or the authorities."

Matthew chimed in, "I can ask around the docks, casual-like. Fishermen hear all sorts of things."

"We'll get to the bottom of this," Sarah said, her voice steady with newfound determination. "Whatever's going on, we'll uncover it."

Mr Thorne placed a hand on her shoulder, his touch

conveying both pride and caution. "Just be careful, both of you. We don't know who might be involved or how deep this goes."

As Sarah looked out over the vast expanse of sea, the familiar sight now held new mysteries. The lighthouse's role in protecting sailors took on a deeper meaning. She was no longer just tending the light; she was guardian of a truth that could save lives.

∼

'Lady Isabel' was now a haunting sight. The once-proud merchant ship now lay partially submerged, its broken hull a jagged silhouette against the rocks. The setting sun cast long shadows across the water, transforming the wreck into an eerie monument to the day's events.

A chill ran down Sarah's spine as she contemplated the whispered words of sabotage and the captain's bewildered expression. The peaceful coastal waters she'd grown to love now seemed to hide treacherous secrets beneath their placid surface.

"We can't let this go," she murmured, her voice barely audible above the distant crash of waves.

Matthew nodded, his good hand clenching into a fist. "We won't. Whatever's going on, with God's help we'll figure it out."

Sarah's resolve hardened like steel forged in fire. The enormity of what they faced was daunting, but she felt a fierce determination take root. This was about more than just one shipwreck; it was about protecting the town she loved and the sailors who depended on the safety of these waters.

As darkness fell, Mr Thorne lit the lighthouse lamp. Sarah watched as the powerful beam began its nightly vigil, sweeping across the sea in a steady, unwavering rhythm. To her, it seemed to embody their commitment – a beacon of truth cutting through the darkness of deception.

"We'll need to be careful," Sarah said, turning to Matthew.

"Keep our eyes and ears open, just like Mr Thorne said. Every conversation, every odd behaviour could be a clue."

Matthew's eyes gleamed with a mix of excitement and apprehension. "It's like we're detectives now, isn't it? But with real danger."

Sarah nodded. "Real danger, and real consequences if we fail."

A CRUMBLING CALM

~~~

*I*t had been three months since the 'Lady Isabel' incident, and the tranquillity of Weymouth's coastline had been shattered by a series of inexplicable shipwrecks.

"Anything amiss?" Mr Thorne's gruff voice called from below.

Sarah shook her head, though her brow remained furrowed. "Not yet. But after the 'Mermaid's Tear' last week..."

She didn't need to finish. They both knew the grim tally: five ships in as many months, all running aground in weather that any seasoned captain should have navigated with ease.

Down in the harbour, Matthew Fletcher coiled rope on his father's fishing boat, his movements tense and distracted. The once-bustling docks were eerily quiet, with fewer vessels setting out each day.

"Ain't natural," old Tom grumbled from the next berth over. "Clear skies, calm seas, and ships still finding rocks? Someone's playin' us for fools."

Matthew nodded, his jaw clenched. He'd heard the whispers, seen the fearful glances. Weymouth was changing, and not for the better.

In the marketplace, Mrs Hawkins' usually cheerful face was pinched with worry as she arranged her vegetables. "Did you hear about the 'Siren's Call'?" she murmured to Miss Havisham, who had come down for supplies. "Ran aground just last night. In weather clear as crystal, they say."

"Something's not right," a grizzled sailor muttered nearby to his crew mate, ship rocking beneath them as they worked. "Ain't no coincidence, all these wrecks. Mark my words, there's dark work afoot."

The once-thriving harbour town now felt like a powder keg, ready to ignite at the slightest spark.

～

SARAH CAMPBELL'S fingers trembled as she recorded yet another entry in the lighthouse logbook. The 'Siren's Call' – the sixth wreck in as many months. Her neat handwriting belied the turmoil churning within her.

She spread out the nautical maps across the desk, her brow furrowed in concentration. Weather reports lay scattered around her, each one telling the same story – clear skies, calm seas. It made no sense.

"There has to be an explanation," Sarah muttered, tracing the coastline with her finger.

Her light blue eyes, once bright with enthusiasm for her duties, now held a storm of worry. She found herself at the telescope more often than not, scanning the waters with an intensity that left her vision blurry.

Mr Thorne's footsteps echoed up the spiral staircase. "Any changes, Sarah?"

She shook her head, not taking her eyes off the horizon. "Nothing yet. But I can't shake this feeling..."

He placed a reassuring hand on her shoulder. "You're doing all you can, lass. Sometimes the sea keeps her secrets."

But Sarah couldn't accept that. Each morning, she rose before dawn, determined to unravel the mystery. She checked and rechecked the light, ensuring its beam cut through even the faintest mist. Her eyes constantly darted between the logbook, the maps, and the vast expanse of water beyond the lighthouse windows.

As the sun climbed higher, Sarah found herself perched at the top of the lighthouse, telescope in hand. She knew every rock, every current, every trick of light on the water. Yet somehow, ships kept meeting their doom on Weymouth's shores.

SHADOWS IN THE HARBOUR

The sun had long since dipped below the waves, leaving behind a sky painted in deep purples and blues, painting the harbour in a normally beautiful hue. Tonight though, it felt like an imposing omen to Sarah. The air was thick with the scent of salt and seaweed, mingling with the lingering odour of smoke from the day's rescue efforts.

Sarah heard the crunch of gravel behind her and turned to see Matthew approaching. His broad shoulders were slumped with exhaustion, his usually tanned face pale in the fading light. Sarah's heart clenched at the sight of him, knowing he'd been out on the water all day, helping with 'Siren Call's' rescue.

"Matthew," she called softly, her voice carrying over the lapping waves.

He joined her at the water's edge. For a moment, they stood in silence, both lost in their own thoughts.

Sarah took a deep breath, steeling herself. "It's happening too often, Matthew. These wrecks... they're not right."

She turned to face him, her eyes meeting his. In the dim light, she could see the concern etched on his face, mirroring her own.

"I've been keeping track," she continued, her voice trembling slightly. "The patterns, the weather, the timing... it doesn't make sense."

Matthew listened intently, his brow furrowing as Sarah spoke. She detailed her observations, the fear in her voice growing with each word.

"It's as if... as if someone is luring these ships to their doom," she whispered, the words hanging heavy in the air between them.

Matthew's hand found hers, squeezing gently. "I trust your judgment. You know these waters better than anyone."

Sarah nodded, grateful for his unwavering support. "I can't shake this feeling, Matthew. Something sinister is at work here, and I'm afraid for our town, for the sailors... for all of us."

Matthew's eyes hardened with determination. "We'll get to the bottom of this, Sarah. Together. Keep digging, keep watching."

Sarah's eyes darted around the harbour, scanning for any eavesdroppers. Satisfied they were alone, she tugged Matthew's sleeve, guiding him towards a secluded nook between two weathered fishing boats. The smell of tar and damp wood enveloped them as they huddled close.

"We need a plan," Sarah breathed, her heart racing.

Matthew nodded. "Agreed. But where do we start? It's not like we can just walk up to the harbourmaster and demand answers."

Sarah chewed her lower lip, her mind racing. Suddenly, her eyes lit up. "The survivors! We should talk to the captains and crews from the wrecked ships. They might have noticed something odd before disaster struck."

"Brilliant," Matthew whispered. "I know some of them are staying at The Rusty Anchor while their ships are being repaired. We could start there."

Sarah nodded eagerly, but then furrowed her brow. "That's a

good start, but I can't shake the feeling there's more to this. What if..." She paused, choosing her words carefully. "What if we looked into the shipping logs and cargo manifests?"

Matthew raised an eyebrow. "You think there might be discrepancies?"

"It's possible," Sarah replied urgently. "If someone's deliberately wrecking ships, there might be a pattern in the cargo they're carrying. Or maybe the logs don't match up with what actually happened."

Matthew's eyes widened with understanding. "That's clever, Sarah. But how do we get access to those documents?"

Sarah's mind raced, considering their options. "I might be able to convince Mr Thorne to request them from the harbourmaster. He could say it's for lighthouse records or something."

"It's risky," Matthew whispered, his eyes darting around the harbour. "But you're right. We need to know what's in those logs."

Sarah nodded, her mind already racing ahead. "I'll speak to Mr Thorne tonight."

Matthew squeezed her hand, his touch sending a flutter through her chest despite the gravity of the situation. "Be careful, Sarah. We don't know who might be involved in this."

Sarah's eyes met his, fierce determination burning in their depths. "I will be. But we can't stand by and do nothing. Too many lives are at stake."

As they emerged from their hiding spot, Sarah caught sight of a figure stumbling along the harbour's edge. She recognized him instantly – Captain Everett of the ill-fated 'Lady Isabel'. His once-proud posture was now hunched, his face haggard and drawn.

"Look," Sarah whispered, nudging Matthew. "There's our chance to start gathering information."

They approached the captain cautiously. Up close, Sarah

could see the haunted look in his eyes, the tremor in his hands as he clutched a half-empty bottle.

"Captain Everett?" Sarah called softly. "Are you all right?"

The man's bloodshot eyes fixed on her, recognition slowly dawning. "You... you were there. When we wrecked."

Sarah nodded, her voice gentle. "Yes, sir. We helped with the rescue. We were hoping we could ask you a few questions about what happened that day."

Captain Everett's face crumpled, a mix of grief and something Sarah couldn't quite place – was it guilt? – flashing across his features. "It was impossible," he muttered, more to himself than to them. "Clear skies, calm seas... and then..."

He trailed off, his gaze drifting back to the bottle in his hand. Sarah exchanged a quick glance with Matthew, silently urging him to press further.

"Captain," Matthew said softly, placing a gentle hand on the man's trembling arm. "Can you tell us more about what happened? Anything you remember might help prevent future accidents."

The captain's bloodshot eyes met his, filled with a torment that made Sarah's chest tighten. He took a shaky breath, his knuckles whitening around the bottle.

"It was as if... as if the ship had a mind of its own," he muttered. "One moment, we were on course. The next..." He shuddered, taking a long pull from the bottle.

"Did you notice anything unusual before the ship veered off course?" Matthew pressed. "Any strange lights, sounds, or movements in the water?"

Captain Everett's brow furrowed, his gaze distant as if reliving those fateful moments. "Nothing. Everything was fine. We had had some issues with some of our instruments during the voyage, but I'd been assured they were all taken care of…"

He trailed off, and it was clear he had no more to say. Sarah and Matthew took their leave of him, and agreed to start their investigations in earnest.

THREADS OF EVIDENCE

The next day, Sarah and Matthew made their way through the bustling harbour. The salty air filled her lungs, but it did little to calm her nerves. They had a mission, and it pressed down on her shoulders like a physical thing.

"There," Matthew whispered, nodding towards a group of weathered sailors huddled near a stack of crates. "I recognise a few from 'Siren's Call'."

Sarah nodded, steeling herself. They approached casually, careful not to draw attention. When they were close enough, Sarah cleared her throat softly.

"Excuse me, gentlemen," she said, her voice low but steady. "We were hoping we might have a word with you about... recent events."

The sailors exchanged wary glances, but one – a grizzled man with a greying beard – gave a curt nod. He led them to a quieter spot behind some barrels.

"What do you want to know?" he asked gruffly.

Sarah took a deep breath. "We're trying to understand what happened during the wrecks. Did you notice anything... unusual before disaster struck?"

The old sailor's eyes narrowed, but there was a flicker of something – fear? – behind them. "Aye," he muttered. "There was somethin' off that day."

As they spoke to more survivors, a pattern emerged. Each account added another piece to a puzzling picture. A young deckhand spoke of eerie lights dancing on the rocks just before their ship veered off course. A second mate described holes suddenly appearing in the ship's underbelly, letting water gush in.

With each interview the pieces were starting to fit together, but the picture they formed was more frightening than she had imagined. She caught Matthew's eye, seeing her own mix of determination and unease reflected there.

As they walked away from their last interview, Sarah's mind whirled with possibilities. "Matthew," she whispered, "It seems certain now. These weren't accidents. All these ships were sabotaged!"

Matthew's jaw clenched, his eyes scanning the harbour as if searching for unseen enemies. "I think you might be right, Sarah. But why?"

Sarah shook her head, frustration and fear warring within her. "I don't know. But we need to find out – before more ships are lost."

~

SARAH'S QUILL scratched across the parchment, her brow furrowed in concentration as she carefully transcribed the day's findings. The lighthouse's lantern room, usually a place of quiet vigilance, now buzzed with the energy of their investigation. Matthew sat across from her, his own notes spread before him like a chaotic sea chart.

"It's all here," Sarah murmured, more to herself than to Matthew. "Every account, every strange light, every unexplained leak." Her neat, precise handwriting filled page after page.

Matthew's eyes scanned his own rough scrawl. "Aye, and it's not just the recent wrecks. Look here," he said, pushing a weathered logbook towards her. "I've been marking down every unusual occurrence at sea for the past year. There's a pattern forming, Sarah."

Sarah leaned in, her auburn hair falling forward as she examined Matthew's notes. His fisherman's knowledge added a depth to their investigation she couldn't have achieved alone. Together, they began to cross-reference their findings with official records.

"Pass me that weather report," Sarah said, reaching for a stack of papers. Her fingers danced over the documents, pulling out shipping manifests and tide tables. "If we can match these accounts with the official records, we might find something the authorities missed."

As the sun dipped below the horizon, casting long shadows across the lantern room, Sarah and Matthew worked tirelessly. They pored over maritime charts, marking the locations of each wreck with small red crosses. Weather patterns were scrutinised, shipping routes analysed.

"Look at this," Sarah exclaimed, her finger tracing a line on the chart. "Every wreck occurred on a clear day, with calm seas. That can't be a coincidence."

Matthew leaned in, his shoulder brushing against hers as he examined the chart. "You're right. And look here," he said, pointing to a cluster of red marks. "They're all concentrated in this area, just off the coast."

A chill ran down Sarah's spine as the pieces began to fit together.

Sarah's eyes flickered to Matthew's face, catching the way the lamplight played across his features. She quickly looked away, focusing on the chart before them. Her heart skipped a beat, a feeling she couldn't quite explain washing over her.

"We're making progress," she said, her voice soft in the quiet of the lantern room. "I never thought we'd uncover so much."

Matthew nodded, his brow furrowed in concentration. "Aye, and it's all thanks to your sharp mind, Sarah. I'd be lost without your insights."

Sarah felt a warmth spread through her chest at his words. She'd grown to rely on Matthew's steady presence. As they worked side by side, their shoulders occasionally brushing, Sarah found herself opening up about things she'd never shared before.

"Sometimes," she confessed, "I wonder what my parents would think of all this. Of me, living in a lighthouse, investigating shipwrecks."

Matthew's hand found hers, giving it a gentle squeeze. "They'd be proud, Sarah. How could they not be?"

Their eyes met, and for a moment, Sarah felt as if the world had tilted on its axis. There was something in Matthew's gaze, something warm and inviting that took her breath away for a moment. She held his gaze a moment too long before looking away, her cheeks flushing.

As the days turned to weeks, their investigation continued. They spent long hours together, their conversations flowing from the mysteries of the sea to their deepest hopes and fears. Sarah shared stories of her childhood in the bakery, of the dreams she'd once had and the new ones taking shape.

Matthew, in turn, opened up about his own fears, the legacy of his father weighing heavily on his shoulders. Sarah listened, offering comfort and encouragement, her admiration for his courage growing with each passing day.

One evening, as they pored over their notes, Sarah caught herself staring at Matthew's profile. The determined set of his jaw, the way his eyes sparkled with intelligence and kindness – it stirred something within her, a feeling she wasn't quite ready to name.

THE VANISHING CARGO

Sarah's eyes widened as she pored over the latest shipping manifest. Something didn't add up. She glanced at Matthew, who sat across from her at the small table in the lighthouse keeper's quarters, his brow furrowed in concentration.

"Matthew," she said. "Look at this."

He leaned in, his shoulder brushing against hers as he examined the document. Sarah felt a flutter in her chest at his proximity but pushed the feeling aside, focusing on the task at hand.

"These shipments," she continued, tracing her finger along the list. "They don't match the cargo we saw salvaged from the wrecks. It's as if some items simply vanished."

Matthew's eyes narrowed. "You're right. But where could they have gone?"

Sarah bit her lip, her mind racing. "What if... what if someone's benefiting from these wrecks? It could be..."

"Smuggling," Matthew finished, his voice serious.

They exchanged a look, the weight of their discovery settling over them. Sarah considered the implications.

"We need to dig deeper," she said, determination lacing her words. "There must be a pattern we're missing."

Over the next few days, Sarah and Matthew expanded their investigation. They pored over insurance claims, interviewed dock workers, and even ventured into the seedier parts of Weymouth to gather information.

As they worked, Sarah started noticing small details she'd previously overlooked. A shipment that arrived unexpectedly at the docks. Whispered conversations that ceased abruptly when she approached. The way certain townspeople seemed to prosper despite the recent tragedies.

One evening, as they walked along the harbour, Sarah spotted a group of men unloading crates from a small boat. There was something furtive about their movements, something that didn't sit right with her.

"Matthew," she whispered, tugging at his sleeve. "Look there. Does that seem odd to you?"

He followed her gaze, his body tensing beside her. "Aye, it does. Those crates... they're not marked like the usual shipments."

Sarah's heart raced as they watched the men disappear into a nearby warehouse. She turned to Matthew, her eyes bright with a mix of excitement and apprehension.

"We're onto something," she said, her voice barely containing her excitement. "I can feel it."

∼

Sarah had done her best to keep Mr Thorne up to date and in the loop with all of her and Matthew's finding, and he in turn supplied them with all the documents and reports he could wrangled out of the harbourmaster.

"You've done well, Sarah." Mr Thorne said. "Your observations are astute, and your dedication to uncovering the truth is commendable."

Pride surged through Sarah, but it was quickly tempered by his next statement.

"However," he continued, fixing her with a stern gaze, "this is a dangerous path you're treading. If your suspicions are correct, you may be dealing with individuals who won't hesitate to protect their interests, by any means necessary."

THE WEIGHT OF SECRETS

Another ship had been wrecked, its splintered remains now scattered along the shoreline. Sarah's heart ached as she watched the sailors salvaging what little they could from the wreckage.

She turned her gaze to the town, noticing how the once-bustling streets near the harbour now stood eerily quiet. Shops that had thrived on the maritime trade were shuttered, their owners too afraid to open for fear of bad luck.

At the marketplace, Sarah overheard snippets of worried conversations.

"It's cursed, I tell you," Mrs Hawkins whispered to her neighbour, her eyes darting nervously towards the sea. "The harbour's been hexed by some evil spirit."

"Nonsense," Mr Browning, the grocer, retorted. But his furrowed brow betrayed his own unease. "It's just a string of bad luck. It'll pass."

Sarah's chest tightened as she listened. She knew the truth was far more sinister than curses or bad luck, but she couldn't reveal what she and Matthew had discovered. Not yet.

As if summoned by her thoughts, Matthew appeared at her

side, his face grim. "Another merchant's threatening to leave," he murmured, his voice low. "Says he can't risk losing another shipment."

Sarah nodded, her throat tight. "We're running out of time, Matthew. If this keeps up, Weymouth will be a ghost town by summer's end."

They walked together along the harbour's edge, their secret investigation pressing down on them like lead. Sarah's mind raced, trying to piece together the clues they'd gathered. The discrepancies in the shipping manifests, the mysterious lights reported by survivors, the concentrated area of wrecks – it all pointed to a deliberate scheme. But to what end?

"We need to work faster," Sarah said. "Every day we delay, more lives are put at risk."

Matthew jaw was set with determination. "We will, Sarah. We'll figure this out, I promise."

As they reached the lighthouse, Sarah paused, looking back at the town she'd grown to love. The fear and suspicion hanging over Weymouth was palpable, threatening to tear apart the very fabric of the community. She knew that she and Matthew might be the only ones who could unravel this mystery and save their home.

A DANGEROUS DISCOVERY

Sarah's eyes burned from the strain of poring over countless documents. The lantern room of the lighthouse was littered with papers, shipping logs, and hastily scribbled notes. Matthew sat across from her, his brow furrowed in concentration as he sifted through another stack of records.

"There has to be something we're missing," Sarah muttered, rubbing her tired eyes. She reached for another document, her fingers brushing against a crumpled piece of paper she hadn't noticed before.

"Matthew, look at this," she said, smoothing out the wrinkled sheet. "It was mixed in with the salvage from the 'Mermaid's Whisper'."

Matthew leaned in, his shoulder brushing against hers as they examined the paper together. Sarah's breath caught in her throat as she realised what they were looking at.

"It's... some kind of code," Matthew whispered, his eyes widening.

Sarah's heart began to race as she studied the jumble of letters and numbers. "You're right. And look here," she pointed to a series of symbols at the bottom of the page. "These look like they could be dates."

Matthew's excitement was palpable. "And these could be ship names," he said, indicating another section of the coded message.

As they worked to decipher the code, Sarah felt a mix of exhilaration and dread. Each symbol they cracked revealed more of the sinister plot they'd been investigating.

"Sarah," Matthew's voice was hushed, "this isn't just one person's work. Look at how many different operations are coordinated here."

Sarah nodded, her mouth dry. "It's a network," she whispered. "A whole group of people working together to cause these wrecks."

Their eyes met, the gravity of their discovery settling over them like a heavy fog. Sarah's mind reeled with the implications. Who could be behind such a vast conspiracy? And how deep did it go?

Sarah's heart raced as she and Matthew huddled over the coded message, their heads nearly touching as they pored over the cryptic symbols. The lantern room, usually a place of calm and routine, now thrummed with an electric energy of discovery and danger.

"We can't ignore this, Matthew," Sarah said. "These names, these dates... it's all here."

Matthew nodded. "You're right. We've stumbled onto something big, Sarah. Bigger than we ever imagined."

Sarah stood abruptly, pacing the small circular room. Her mind whirled with possibilities, connections forming like constellations in the night sky. "We need to act on this information, and quickly. But we must be careful."

"Agreed," Matthew said, rising to join her. "What do you propose?"

Sarah turned to face him, her blue eyes alight with purpose.

"We follow these leads. Each name, each shipment mentioned. We track them down, piece by piece."

Matthew's face broke into a grim smile. "It won't be easy. These people, whoever they are, they're organised. Powerful."

"All the more reason to expose them," Sarah countered, her voice gaining strength. "Think of all the lives lost, the families torn apart. We can't stand by and let it continue."

They spent the next hour meticulously planning their next moves. Sarah jotted down names and dates in her neat handwriting, while Matthew sketched out a rough map of Weymouth, marking potential locations of interest.

"We'll need to be discreet," Sarah murmured, glancing towards the lighthouse door. "If anyone suspects what we're doing..."

Matthew placed a reassuring hand on her shoulder. "We'll be careful. Together, we can do this."

Sarah nodded. They were on the brink of uncovering a vast conspiracy, and that knowledge both terrified and emboldened her.

THE GENTLEMAN FROM LONDON

The news of Ethan Blackwood's arrival in Weymouth spread like wildfire through the seaside town. Whispers and excited chatter filled the marketplace, the harbour, and every corner where townsfolk gathered.

"Did you hear? A gentleman from London has come to stay!"

"They say he's as handsome as a prince and twice as rich!"

Sarah overheard these snippets as she made her way through the bustling streets. She couldn't help but notice the flutter of excitement that seemed to ripple through the town, especially among the young ladies.

As she rounded the corner onto the Esplanade, Sarah caught her first glimpse of the man everyone was talking about. Ethan Blackwood cut a striking figure against the backdrop of the sea. His tailored suit and polished shoes gleamed in the sunlight, a stark contrast to the worn clothes of the fishermen and labourers nearby.

Ethan strolled along the promenade, twirling an ornate cane with practiced ease. His dark hair was perfectly coiffed, and a charming smile played on his lips as he tipped his hat to those he passed by. Sarah noticed how the local girls giggled and blushed as he passed, their eyes following his every move.

Mrs Hawkins, the fishmonger's wife, leaned in close to Sarah. "They say he's come for his health, but if you ask me, a man that handsome is bound to be looking for a wife."

Sarah watched as Ethan paused to admire the view, his green eyes scanning the horizon. There was something about him that seemed both alluring and slightly out of place in their modest town.

As if sensing her gaze, Ethan turned and locked eyes with Sarah. For a moment, she felt a jolt of... something. Curiosity? Intrigue? Before she could ponder it further, he flashed her a dazzling smile and continued on his way.

The town buzzed with speculation about Ethan Blackwood's purpose in Weymouth. Some said he was fleeing a scandal in London, others insisted he was scouting for business opportunities. But one thing was certain – his presence had stirred up excitement in the normally quiet seaside community.

Ethan Blackwood took up residence in a grand house near the newly built Weymouth Pavilion. The location couldn't have been more perfect for a man of his standing – close to the heart of the town's burgeoning cultural scene.

It didn't take long for Ethan to become a regular fixture in the local establishments. The Rusty Anchor, once a humble fisherman's pub, now found itself hosting a most distinguished guest. Ethan would often be seen there in the evenings, a glass of fine whiskey in hand, regaling the patrons with tales of London's high society.

"You should see the ballrooms of Mayfair," he'd say, his eyes twinkling with amusement. "Why, the chandeliers alone are worth more than this entire street!"

The locals would lean in, captivated by his every word. Even the most sceptical of the old sea dogs found themselves drawn into Ethan's world of glamour and sophistication.

. . .

AT WENTWORTH'S TEA ROOM, Ethan became something of an afternoon attraction. Ladies would time their visits hoping to catch a glimpse of the handsome newcomer, or better yet, exchange a few words with him.

"In London, afternoon tea is an art form," Ethan would explain, his refined accent in stark contrast to the local Dorset drawl. "The finest china, delicate pastries, and conversation that could make or break a person's social standing."

Mrs Wentworth herself seemed quite taken with their new regular customer. She'd flutter about, ensuring Ethan's tea was always piping hot and his scones freshly baked.

Everywhere Ethan went, he left a trail of whispers and admiring glances in his wake. His immaculate clothing – always the latest London fashion – stood out among the practical attire of Weymouth's residents. Even something as simple as the way he adjusted his cufflinks or smoothed his perfectly coiffed hair became a topic of conversation.

"Did you see how he held his teacup?" one young lady would whisper to another. "So refined!"

"And those boots! I've never seen leather polished to such a shine," a shopkeeper remarked to his wife.

THE NEWCOMER'S CHARM

*S*arah rolled up her sleeves, not afraid to get her hands dirty as she worked alongside the mariners.

"Hand me that wrench, will you, Tom?" she called out, her voice clear and confident over the din of the harbour.

As she tightened a loose bolt, Sarah felt someone's gaze upon her. She glanced up, catching sight of a well-dressed gentleman observing her from the edge of the dock. His eyes seemed to study her intently, a look of curiosity etched across his refined features.

Sarah recognised him as the newcomer everyone in town had been buzzing about – Ethan Blackwood. His presence here at the harbour seemed out of place, his fashionable attire standing out against the rough-and-tumble surroundings.

Mr Hawkins, harbourmaster, approached with Mr Blackwood in tow. "Miss Campbell," he called out, "there's someone here I'd like you to meet."

Sarah wiped her hands on a nearby rag and straightened up, meeting Mr Blackwood's gaze directly. She noticed how his eyes seemed to take in every detail of her appearance, from her work-worn hands to her determined expression.

"Miss Campbell, may I introduce Mr Ethan Blackwood," Mr Hawkins said. "He's new to our little town and has expressed an interest in our maritime affairs."

Sarah extended her hand, her grip firm and assured. "It's a pleasure to meet you, Mr Blackwood. Welcome to Weymouth."

"Thank you, Miss Campbell," Ethan said, his voice smooth and cultured. "I've heard quite a bit about you since arriving in Weymouth. It seems you're something of a local legend."

A blush crept up Sarah's neck. "I wouldn't say that, Mr Blackwood. I simply do my part to keep our shores safe."

Ethan's smile widened. "Ah, but that's precisely what makes you remarkable. Tell me, how did you come to work at the lighthouse?"

As Sarah recounted her story, she found herself drawn in by Ethan's attentiveness. He asked thoughtful questions, his eyes never leaving her face as she spoke. She was surprised by how easy it was to talk to him, despite his obvious sophistication.

"London must seem a world away from our little town," Sarah remarked, curious about his life in the city.

Ethan chuckled, a rich sound that seemed to warm the air around them. "It has its charms, to be sure. But I find there's something refreshing about Weymouth. The sea air, the sense of community... and of course, the fascinating people."

His gaze lingered on Sarah as he said this, causing her heart to skip a beat. She couldn't help but feel flattered by his attention.

"I must say, Miss Campbell," Ethan continued, "I find it admirable how you've taken on such responsibilities. It's not often one sees a woman in such a position, especially one so young. Your intelligence and dedication are truly commendable."

Sarah felt a mix of pride and slight discomfort at his praise. "Thank you, Mr Blackwood. But I assure you, I'm simply doing what needs to be done. The safety of our mariners is paramount."

"I must come and visit you some time at your lighthouse." Ethan said with a smile.

"I would very much like that." Sarah couldn't help but return his smile.

∾

OVER THE NEXT FEW DAYS, Sarah found herself eagerly anticipating Ethan's visits to the lighthouse. Each time he arrived, his arms were laden with books on maritime navigation and tales of London's vibrant life. The familiar stone walls of the lighthouse seemed to expand, filled with the excitement of new knowledge and far-off places.

"You should see the ships coming into the Thames, Miss Campbell," Ethan said one afternoon, his eyes alight with enthusiasm. "Some of them dwarf even our largest vessels here."

Sarah leaned forward, her elbows resting on the rough wooden table as she listened intently. "Tell me more about the innovations you mentioned yesterday," she urged, her light blue eyes reflecting a newfound longing for adventure.

As Ethan described the latest advancements in navigation technology, Sarah's world grew larger with each word. The familiar rhythms of lighthouse life suddenly seemed small in comparison to the bustling world Ethan painted with his stories.

His sophisticated manners and worldly knowledge provided a stark contrast to the life she had always known. Sarah imagined walks along London's grand streets, visiting museums filled with treasures from around the globe.

One evening, as Sarah was recording the day's weather patterns in the logbook, Matthew arrived at the lighthouse. His brow furrowed as he noticed the stack of books Ethan had left behind.

"Sarah," Matthew began hesitantly, "I'm not sure about this Ethan fellow. Something about him doesn't sit right with me."

Sarah looked up from her work, a small frown creasing her forehead. "What do you mean, Matthew? He's been nothing but kind and informative."

Matthew shifted uncomfortably. "I just think you should be careful. We don't know much about him or why he's really here in Weymouth."

Sarah felt a flicker of annoyance at Matthew's words. She gently pushed aside his concerns, her voice soft but firm. "I appreciate your concern, Matthew, but I think you're worrying over nothing. Ethan has been a wonderful friend and has opened my eyes to so much beyond our little town."

Guilt flushed through Sarah as she saw the hurt flash across Matthew's face. She hadn't meant to dismiss his concerns so abruptly, but she couldn't help feeling defensive of her new friendship with Ethan.

"I'm sorry, Matthew," she said, softening her tone. "I know you're just looking out for me. But Ethan has been nothing but polite and helpful. He's shown me so much about the world beyond Weymouth."

Matthew's brow remained furrowed, his dark eyes clouded with worry. "I understand, Sarah. It's just... we've known each other for so long. I thought we were in this investigation together."

Sarah's heart clenched at the hint of betrayal in Matthew's voice. She reached out and placed a gentle hand on his arm. "We are, Matthew. Nothing has changed that. Ethan's stories and knowledge don't change our friendship or our mission to uncover the truth about these shipwrecks."

Matthew's posture relaxed slightly, but a shadow of doubt still lingered in his eyes. "I hope you're right, Sarah. Just... be careful, all right? We still don't know who's behind all this, and newcomers to town should be viewed with caution."

Sarah nodded, acknowledging the wisdom in Matthew's words. "I will be, I promise. Now, why don't you tell me what you've discovered about the shipping manifests we were examining last week?"

As Matthew began to share his findings, Sarah listened intently, pushing thoughts of Ethan to the back of her mind. The familiar rhythm of their collaboration settled over them. Whatever excitement Ethan brought to her life, she knew that her true calling lay here, in unravelling the mystery that threatened her beloved Weymouth.

A NIGHT AT THE PAVILION

Sarah held Ethan's invitation in her hands, the elegant script promising an evening of culture and excitement at the Weymouth Pavilion. She hesitated, her fingers tracing the embossed edges of the card. The thought of stepping into such a grand affair made her stomach twist with a mix of excitement and trepidation.

"It's just one night," Ethan had said, his green eyes twinkling with charm. "A chance to see a bit of the world beyond the lighthouse."

His words echoed in her mind as she stood before the small mirror in her room, smoothing down the front of her dress. It was a modest gown, but the nicest she owned, with a delicate lace collar and a deep blue hue that brought out the colour of her eyes.

Her hands trembled slightly as she pinned up her auburn hair, trying to mimic the fashionable styles she'd seen in town. She'd never attended such a grand event before, and the thought of being surrounded by Weymouth's elite made her palms sweat.

A gentle knock at the door startled her from her thoughts. "Come in," she called.

Mr Thorne entered, his weathered face softening as he took in the sight of her. "You look lovely, Sarah," he said, his gruff voice tinged with a hint of pride and concern.

Sarah managed a small smile, grateful for his presence. "Thank you, Mr Thorne. I... I'm not sure I belong at such a fancy affair."

Mr Thorne stepped closer, placing a reassuring hand on her shoulder. "You belong wherever you choose to be, Sarah. Just..." he paused, choosing his words carefully. "Just remember who you are. The lighthouse doesn't stop guiding ships just because there are brighter lights in town."

Sarah nodded. She took a deep breath, squaring her shoulders as she faced her reflection once more. The girl in the mirror looked both familiar and strange – a curious blend of the lighthouse keeper's assistant and a young woman on the cusp of something new.

∽

As she stepped into the grand hall of the Weymouth Pavilion, Sarah had to take a moment to catch her breath. Her hand was resting lightly on Ethan's proffered arm. The opulence of the scene was overwhelming – crystal chandeliers sparkled overhead, casting a warm glow across the polished wooden floors where elegantly dressed couples twirled to the strains of a string quartet.

She felt acutely aware of her modest gown, feeling inadequate in comparison to the silk and satin that adorned the other ladies. But Ethan's reassuring smile bolstered her confidence as he guided her further into the room.

"My dear," Ethan said, his voice smooth as velvet, "allow me to introduce you to some of Weymouth's finest." He steered her towards a group of distinguished-looking gentlemen engaged in animated conversation.

"Mr Hargrave, Captain Leighton," Ethan called out, catching their attention. "May I present Miss Sarah Campbell?"

Sarah curtsied, feeling their appraising gazes. Mr Reginald Hargrave, a tall man with greying ginger hair and an imposing presence, nodded curtly. His stern demeanour sent a shiver down Sarah's spine, though she couldn't quite place why.

"Ah, the lighthouse girl," Captain Jonathan Leighton said, his wrinkle-laden face breaking into a smile that didn't quite reach his eyes. "I've heard talk of your dedication to keeping our shores safe."

Sarah opened her mouth to respond, but found herself momentarily speechless. The grandeur of the Pavilion and the unfamiliar faces pressed in on her. She took a steadying breath, reminding herself of Mr Thorne's words. She belonged here as much as anyone else.

"Thank you, Captain," she finally managed, her voice growing stronger with each word. "The safety of our mariners is of utmost importance to me."

A flutter of nerves passed over Sarah as she stood among these influential men, but Ethan's steady presence beside her helped calm her racing heart. She watched in awe as he effortlessly guided the conversation, his charm and wit drawing everyone in.

"Miss Campbell," Mr Hargrave said, his voice deep and commanding, "I understand you assist Mr Thorne at the lighthouse. How do you find the work?"

Sarah straightened her shoulders, determined to make a good impression. "It's challenging but rewarding, sir. Every day brings new lessons about the sea and the importance of vigilance."

Captain Leighton nodded approvingly. "Good to hear. A

steady hand at the lighthouse can make all the difference between life and death out there."

Ethan smoothly interjected, "Sarah's dedication is truly admirable. I've had the pleasure of visiting the lighthouse, and her knowledge is quite impressive."

Sarah glanced at Ethan gratefully, marvelling at how easily he manoeuvred through these social waters.

As the conversation flowed, Sarah was both fascinated and slightly intimidated by the men around her. They spoke of politics, business ventures, and social connections – a world far removed from her own simple life. Yet, Ethan made sure to include her, often asking for her opinion or relating topics back to her experiences.

"And what do you think of the recent developments in Weymouth, Miss Campbell?" Mr Hargrave asked, his piercing gaze fixed on her. "I hear there's been some... unrest among the locals."

Sarah hesitated, acutely aware of the delicate nature of the topic. She thought of the tensions she'd witnessed in the marketplace, the whispers of discontent. But before she could formulate a response, Ethan smoothly stepped in.

"I'm sure Sarah has a unique perspective, given her connections to both the old and new Weymouth," he said, giving her hand a reassuring squeeze. "Perhaps we could discuss it over a dance? The music is quite enticing."

With a polite nod to the gentlemen, Ethan led Sarah towards the dance floor, saving her from the uncomfortable question. As they moved away, Sarah felt an admiration for Ethan's social grace.

Ethan guided her through the intricate steps of the dance. His hand on her waist felt warm and reassuring, steadying her as they moved across the polished floor. The music swelled around them, and Sarah was swept up in the moment, her earlier nervousness melting away.

As they twirled, Ethan leaned in close, his breath tickling her ear. "You're doing splendidly, my dear," he murmured. "I daresay you'd fit right in at any London ball."

"Oh, I doubt that," she said with a small laugh. "I'm sure I'd be quite out of place among all those grand ladies and gentlemen."

Ethan's eyes sparkled with amusement. "Nonsense," he declared. "Why, just last month, I attended a soirée at the Duchess of Marlborough's townhouse. The conversation there was nowhere near as stimulating as our chats about your lighthouse work."

As the dance ended, Ethan led Sarah to a quiet corner of the room. There, he regaled her with tales of London's high society, each story more captivating than the last. He spoke of glittering ballrooms where diamonds sparkled like stars, of witty exchanges in smoky gentlemen's clubs, and of intellectual salons where the greatest minds of the age debated philosophy and politics.

Sarah listened, utterly enthralled. Her eyes widened with wonder as Ethan described a world so different from her own. She could almost see the grand mansions of Mayfair, smell the perfumed air of a duchess's drawing room, hear the clever repartee of lords and ladies.

"And then," Ethan said, his smooth laughter filling the air, "Lord Ashbury's wig caught fire from the candelabra! You should have seen the poor man's face as he tried to maintain his dignity while his valet doused him with a glass of champagne!"

Sarah couldn't help but join in his laughter, the sound of their combined mirth drawing curious glances from nearby guests. For a moment, she forgot about the lighthouse, about the shipwrecks, about all the responsibilities that weighed on her shoulders. In that instant, she was simply a young woman enjoying the company of a charming gentleman, caught up in the magic of an enchanting evening.

THE GLINT OF RIVALRY

$\mathscr{D}$

Sarah stepped out onto the Pavilion's balcony, the cool night air a welcome respite from the warmth of the crowded ballroom. She leaned against the railing, her eyes drawn to the familiar silhouette of the Esplanade and the vast expanse of sea beyond. The moon cast a silvery path across the water, reminding her of the countless nights she'd spent watching over these same waters from the lighthouse.

The gentle lapping of waves against the shore mingled with the muffled sounds of music and laughter from inside. Sarah closed her eyes, inhaling deeply. The salty tang of the sea air grounded her in comparison to the heady perfumes and cigar smoke that permeated the ballroom.

"Ah, there you are," Ethan's smooth voice broke through her reverie. She turned to see him approaching, two glasses of champagne in hand. "I thought you might appreciate some fresh air."

Sarah accepted the offered glass with a grateful smile. "Thank you. It's all a bit... overwhelming in there."

Ethan nodded, his eyes twinkling with understanding. "Indeed. But you've handled yourself admirably, my dear. You have a natural grace that many of those so-called ladies of society would envy."

He joined her at the railing, his gaze sweeping over the moonlit bay. "You know, Sarah," he began, his voice taking on a passionate tone, "I can't help but think of the opportunities that await someone like you. Your intellect, your spirit – they're wasted in this small town."

Sarah's heart quickened at his words. Ethan turned to face her fully, his eyes alight with enthusiasm. "Just imagine the adventures you could have, the people you could meet, the difference you could make in the world. London, Paris, New York – the possibilities are endless for a woman of your calibre."

His words painted a vivid picture in Sarah's mind. She saw herself strolling through bustling city streets, attending lectures at grand universities, perhaps even working alongside renowned scientists and inventors. The image was intoxicating, filled with promise and excitement.

Yet, even as her heart swelled with the possibility of these new horizons, Sarah felt a gentle tug of hesitation. Her gaze drifted back to the sea, to the faint pinprick of light that marked the South Point Lighthouse. It stood as a silent reminder of her responsibilities, her past, and the mystery she had yet to solve.

~

MATTHEW FLETCHER STOOD on the docks, his weathered hands gripping a coil of rope as he watched the glittering lights of the Weymouth Pavilion in the distance. The sea breeze ruffled his dark hair, carrying the faint strains of music and laughter from the grand ball. His eyes, usually warm and inviting, now held a troubled look as he caught sight of two figures on the balcony.

Even from afar, he recognised Sarah's graceful silhouette, her auburn hair catching the moonlight. Beside her stood Ethan Blackwood, his tall frame leaning close to Sarah as they conversed. Matthew's stomach twisted, a feeling he couldn't quite place settling in his chest.

He'd known Sarah for years, watched her grow from a grief-stricken child into a capable young woman. They'd shared countless moments on these very docks, discussing their dreams and fears. But now, seeing her in that elegant gown, laughing at something Ethan said, Matthew felt as if she were slipping away.

"Oi, Fletcher! You gonna stand there all night?" called out one of his fellow fishermen.

Matthew shook his head, forcing himself to focus on the task at hand. But as he worked, his mind kept drifting back to Sarah and Ethan. He couldn't help but wonder what they were talking about, what promises of grandeur Ethan might be making.

Protectiveness washed over Matthew. He knew the dangers that lurked in Weymouth's shadows, the mysteries they'd been unravelling together. Did Ethan know about the shipwrecks? About the coded messages and the conspiracy they'd uncovered? Matthew doubted it.

As he hauled in the day's catch, Matthew's thoughts churned like the sea beneath his feet. He wanted Sarah to be happy, to have all the opportunities she deserved. But something about Ethan set him on edge. The man was too polished, too perfect. And the way Sarah looked at him...

Matthew's grip tightened on the fishing net, his knuckles turning white. He realised, with a start, that he was jealous. The feeling sat uncomfortably in his chest, foreign and confusing. Sarah was his friend, his partner in their clandestine investigation. When had she become something more?

THE ALLURE OF NEW HORIZONS

Sarah and Ethan strolled along the moonlit Esplanade. The grand party at the Weymouth Pavilion had been a whirlwind of excitement, leaving her dizzy with new experiences and emotions. Ethan's arm, linked through hers, felt both thrilling and comforting.

"I must say, Miss Campbell, you were the belle of the ball tonight," Ethan said, his voice warm with admiration. "I daresay even the most seasoned London socialites would have been impressed by your grace."

A blush crept across Sarah's cheeks, thankful for the darkness that hid it. "You're too kind, Mr Blackwood. I fear I was more akin to a fish out of water."

Ethan chuckled, a rich sound that sent a shiver down Sarah's spine. "Nonsense. You were a natural. The way you captivated Mr Hargraves with your knowledge of maritime affairs was nothing short of remarkable."

They paused at the harbour's edge, the gentle lapping of waves against the shore a soothing counterpoint to the evening's excitement. Sarah gazed out at the sea, the familiar beacon of South Point Lighthouse blinking in the distance.

"It's a beautiful night," she murmured, suddenly aware of how close Ethan stood beside her.

"Indeed it is," Ethan replied, his eyes fixed not on the horizon, but on Sarah's face. "Though I find myself captivated by a different sort of beauty."

Sarah's breath caught in her throat. She turned to face him, finding his intense gaze both exhilarating and unnerving. "Mr Blackwood, I—"

"Ethan, please," he interrupted gently. "After the evening we've shared, I think we can dispense with formalities, don't you?"

Sarah nodded, a small smile playing at her lips. "Ethan," she repeated, savouring the intimacy of his name on her tongue.

As they resumed their walk, Sarah was torn between the comfort of her familiar world and the exciting possibilities Ethan represented. His stories of London, of grand theatres and bustling streets, so vivid she could almost taste it.

"You know, Sarah," Ethan said as they neared the lighthouse, "I meant what I said earlier. You have a remarkable mind. It would be a shame to see it confined to this small corner of the world."

Sarah's heart fluttered at his words, even as a pang of guilt shot through her. "Weymouth is my home," she said softly. "The lighthouse, Mr Thorne, they're my family now."

Ethan nodded, his expression understanding. "Of course. But family doesn't mean you can't spread your wings, does it? Think of the adventures you could have, the people you could meet, the difference you could make in the world."

Ethan had taken his leave once they had reached the lighthouse door, and Sarah had watched him disappear into the inky black night.

Sarah let events of the evening play out behind her closed eyes like a fevered dream as she lay awake in her bed – the glittering chandeliers of the Weymouth Pavilion, the swish of silk gowns, the intoxicating laughter of the elite.

And Ethan. Always Ethan.

His words echoed in her ears, painting vivid pictures of a life so different from her own, and yet, Sarah at the centre of it all. She could almost feel the pulse of a world beyond the confines of Weymouth.

But with each thrilling image came a pang of guilt. She thought of Mr Thorne, his gruff kindness a constant in her life since that terrible day she lost her parents. The lighthouse itself, solid and dependable, had become more than just a home – it was a purpose, a calling.

Sarah turned restlessly, her blanket tangling around her legs. The memory of Ethan's touch on her arm sent a shiver through her that had nothing to do with the cool night air. His green eyes, so full of admiration and promise, seemed to see something in her that she barely recognised in herself.

"You have a remarkable mind," he had said. The words made her heart flutter even now. Was it true? Could she really make a difference beyond the shores of Weymouth?

But then another face swam into view – Matthew's. Dear, steady Matthew, with his callused hands and honest brown eyes. Matthew, who had stood by her through every investigation, every triumph and setback. The thought of leaving him behind caused an ache within her that she couldn't quite explain.

Sarah sighed, turning once more to stare out the window at the vast, dark sea. The world suddenly seemed so much larger, full of possibilities she had never dared to imagine. Yet here she was, caught between the familiar comfort of her life at the lighthouse and the thrilling unknown Ethan represented.

The future, once so clear, now stretched before her like an uncharted sea, full of promise and peril in equal measure.

A TASTE OF SOPHISTICATION

In the days that followed, Sarah was swept up in a whirlwind of excitement. Ethan's presence in Weymouth had brought a touch of London sophistication to the seaside town, and Sarah couldn't help but be drawn to it. Each morning, she awoke with a flutter of anticipation, wondering what new adventure the day might bring.

Ethan seemed to have an endless supply of invitations. One afternoon, he escorted her along the Esplanade, his arm linked through hers as they strolled past the colourful bathing machines and elegant hotels. Sarah marvelled at how different the familiar sights looked through Ethan's eyes, as if she were seeing them for the first time.

"You must come to the theatre with me tonight," Ethan said, his green eyes twinkling. "There's a traveling company performing 'The Importance of Being Earnest.' I daresay you'll find it most amusing."

Sarah hesitated, thinking of her duties. But Ethan's enthusiasm was infectious, and she found herself nodding in agreement.

The theatre was a revelation. Sarah sat enraptured, drinking in the witty dialogue and the elegant costumes. Ethan leaned close during the performance, whispering explanations of the more sophisticated jokes in her ear. His breath warm against her skin sent shivers down her spine.

Yet, for all the excitement Ethan brought, Sarah couldn't shake a lingering unease. It was like a pebble in her shoe, small but persistent. She pushed the feeling aside, focusing instead on the thrill of new experiences.

Amidst the whirlwind of Ethan's attentions, Matthew remained a steady presence in Sarah's life. His quiet strength was a balm to her sometimes overwhelmed senses. One afternoon, as they mended nets together at the harbour, Sarah poured out her conflicted feelings.

"It's all so grand, Matthew," she said, her hands working the familiar knots. "Ethan speaks of London as if it's some magical place where anything is possible. But then I look at the lighthouse, at you and Mr Thorne, and I wonder..."

Matthew's hands stilled on the net. "You belong wherever you choose to be, Sarah," he said softly. "Don't let anyone else decide that for you."

His words stayed with Sarah as she climbed the lighthouse steps that evening. Mr Thorne was waiting in the lantern room, his weathered face creased with concern.

"You've been out and about quite a bit lately," he said, his tone carefully neutral.

Sarah nodded, suddenly feeling like a child caught in some mischief. "Ethan's been showing me so many new things," she said. "It's as if the world's grown larger overnight."

Mr Thorne's eyes softened. "The world's always been large, lass. It's you that's growing to see it."

HIDDEN IN PLAIN SIGHT

❦

*S*arah leaned over the lighthouse table, she traced a finger along the coastline of a worn map. Beside her, Matthew shuffled through a stack of shipping logs, his eyes darting back and forth as he compared dates and cargo manifests.

The lantern room was bathed in a warm, flickering light, casting long shadows across the scattered papers and documents that covered every available surface. Outside, the rhythmic sweep of the lighthouse beam cut through the darkness.

"Look here," Matthew said, his voice low. He pushed a crumpled piece of paper towards Sarah. "Another coded message. This one mentions the 'Lady Isabel' by name."

Sarah's eyes widened as she scanned the cryptic text. "And the date... it's three days before the wreck. Matthew, this is proof that it was planned!"

They exchanged a look of grim satisfaction. For weeks, they had been piecing together fragments of information, following hunches and whispered rumours. Now, finally, the puzzle was starting to take shape.

Sarah reached for a notebook filled with her meticulous observations. "If we cross-reference this with the patterns we've noticed in the shipping routes..." She trailed off, her mind racing ahead of her words.

Matthew nodded, already on the same wavelength. He pulled out a chart marked with the locations of recent wrecks. "It's not just about the ships that sink," he said slowly. "It's about the ones that don't."

Sarah felt a chill run down her spine as the realisation hit her. "A smuggling operation," she breathed. "Using the wrecks as a cover. From the looks of it, the crash sites allow for the riskier items to be smuggled. But they're double dipping! Because all the attention is on the wrecks, they can send other ships clean through without notice as well!"

The enormity of their discovery settled over them like a heavy fog. This was no longer just about mysterious shipwrecks or local superstitions. They were uncovering a vast conspiracy that reached far beyond the shores of Weymouth. It seemed like this smuggling ring was dealing in all sorts: alcohol, tobacco, and, most terrifying of all to Sarah, weapons.

Matthew's jaw clenched, determination hardening his features. "We need to find out who's behind this, Sarah. And we need to stop them."

Sarah nodded, trepidation coursing through her veins. "It won't be easy," she said. "Whoever's orchestrating this has power and influence. We'll be going up against forces we can't even imagine."

But as she looked at the evidence spread before them, at the fruit of their tireless investigation, Sarah's resolve strengthened. This was bigger than her, bigger than Matthew, bigger than Weymouth itself. But it was a fight they had to take on.

Sarah smoothed her borrowed gown, feeling out of place among the opulent surroundings of the Georgian mansion. Matthew stood beside her, looking equally uncomfortable in his best suit. They exchanged a nervous glance before stepping into the grand ballroom.

Crystal chandeliers cast a warm glow over the gathered elite of Weymouth. Ladies in silk dresses twirled with gentlemen in tailored coats, their laughter mingling with the strains of a string quartet. Sarah took a deep breath, reminding herself of their purpose.

"Remember," she whispered to Matthew, "we're here to observe and listen. Don't draw attention to yourself."

Matthew's eyes were already scanning the room. "I'll mingle near the refreshments. You try to get close to Hargrave and Leighton."

Sarah made her way through the crowd, accepting a glass of champagne from a passing waiter in the way she had seen Ethan do so. She sipped it slowly, her gaze settling on Reginald Hargrave, who stood near the fireplace in deep conversation with a group of gentlemen.

Summoning her courage, Sarah approached, timing her arrival to coincide with a lull in the conversation. "Mr Hargrave," she said, dipping into a curtsy. "What a pleasure to see you again."

Hargrave turned, his eyebrows rising slightly in recognition. "Ah, Miss Campbell. I trust you're enjoying the evening?"

"Indeed, sir. Though I must admit, I find myself quite curious about the recent changes in our little town. I've heard whispers of new business ventures. Perhaps you might enlighten me?"

A flicker of something—wariness?—passed across Hargrave's face before he smiled smoothly. "My dear, the world of business is hardly a topic for such a delightful gathering. But I assure you, Weymouth's future is bright."

Sarah nodded, careful to keep her expression neutral. "Of course. I only hope that our traditional industries, like fishing, won't suffer as a result of progress."

Before Hargrave could respond, Jonathan Leighton joined their circle. "Progress is inevitable, Miss Campbell," he said, his voice gruff but not unkind. "But rest assured, the sea will always be Weymouth's lifeblood."

Sarah studied Leighton's weathered face, searching for any hint of deception. "You would know better than most, Captain. Have you noticed any... unusual activity on the waters lately?"

Leighton's eyes narrowed almost imperceptibly. "Nothing out of the ordinary, Miss Campbell. The sea has its moods, as always."

As the conversation continued, Sarah remained alert, cataloguing every reaction, every nuance of speech. She knew that somewhere in this room, hidden behind polite smiles and casual banter, lay the answers they sought. It was up to her and Matthew to uncover them, no matter how deeply they were buried.

THE RUSTY ANCHOR

Sarah's heart skipped as she and Matthew approached The Rusty Anchor, the first of the seedy taverns they planned to investigate. The salty air mingled with the stench of stale beer and tobacco smoke, growing stronger as they neared the weathered wooden door.

Matthew placed a reassuring hand on her arm. "Stay close," he murmured. "These places can be rough."

Sarah nodded. As they entered, the cacophony of drunken laughter and heated arguments assaulted her ears. Dim oil lamps cast long shadows across the room, revealing grimy tables and a motley assortment of patrons.

Matthew led them to the bar, where a grizzled man with a scar across his cheek eyed them suspiciously. "Two ales," Matthew said, his voice gruff and assured. Sarah marvelled at how easily he slipped into this world, so different from the gentle fisherman she knew.

As they sipped their drinks, Sarah strained to catch snippets of conversation around them. A group of sailors in the corner spoke in hushed tones about a shipment coming in next week.

At another table, a man with an eye patch complained bitterly about "those fancy boys up at the pavilion."

Sarah leaned closer to Matthew. "We need to get them talking," she whispered.

Matthew nodded, then raised his voice slightly. "Heard there was trouble out on the water last night. Anyone know what happened?"

A few heads turned their way. An old sailor with a scraggly beard grunted, "Aye, another ship gone down. They're saying it was the rocks, but I've never known a captain fool enough to sail so close in clear weather."

Sarah's pulse quickened. This was the kind of information they needed. She opened her mouth to ask another question when a familiar voice cut through the din.

"My friends! What a pleasure to find you here."

Sarah turned to see Ethan Blackwood striding towards them, looking impossibly elegant amid the tavern's grime. His presence immediately changed the atmosphere, drawing curious and suspicious glances from the patrons.

"Mr Blackwood," Sarah said, struggling to keep the surprise from her voice. "What brings you to this... establishment?"

Ethan's eyes twinkled. "Oh, I find these old taverns quite fascinating. So much history, so many stories. In fact, I've just heard the most interesting tale about a ship that vanished without a trace last month. Perhaps we could discuss it over a drink?"

Ethan joined them at the bar. His unexpected presence threw her carefully laid plans into disarray. She glanced at Matthew, noting the tightness in his jaw as he nodded a curt greeting to Ethan.

"A vanishing ship, you say?" Sarah asked, striving to keep her voice casual. "That does sound intriguing."

Ethan leaned in conspiratorially. "Oh, indeed. It seems this vessel was carrying quite the valuable cargo when it disappeared. Some whisper of foul play, but who can say for certain?"

Sarah's mind whirled. Could this be connected to the wrecks they'd been investigating? She struggled to maintain her composure, acutely aware of the rough crowd around them.

"What sort of cargo?" Matthew asked, his tone gruff but curious.

Ethan's eyes glinted in the dim light. "Now, that's the real mystery, isn't it? Some say it was gold, others claim it was something far more... exotic."

The old sailor with the scraggly beard snorted. "Exotic, my foot. It's them smugglers, mark my words. Been operating right under our noses for years."

Sarah's breath caught. She exchanged a quick glance with Matthew, seeing her own excitement mirrored in his eyes. This was exactly the kind of information they'd hoped to uncover.

Ethan raised an eyebrow. "Smugglers? In our quaint little Weymouth? Surely not."

The sailor spat on the floor. "You'd be surprised, young master. There's more goes on in these waters than meets the eye."

Sarah leaned forward, her curiosity overcoming her caution. "What do you mean? Have you seen something?"

The sailor's rheumy eyes narrowed. "Seen plenty. But a man's got to be careful what he says these days. Never know who might be listening."

"What sort of things have you seen?" Sarah pressed. She knew she was treading on dangerous ground, but the need for answers outweighed her caution.

The sailor's eyes darted around the tavern, as if searching for unseen listeners. He leaned in, his breath reeking of cheap spirits. "Lights where there shouldn't be lights. Boats movin' about in the dead of night. And them fancy folk from up the hill, comin' down here and askin' questions they've no business askin'."

Sarah's mind whirled with possibilities. Could some of Weymouth's elite be involved in the smuggling ring? She thought of Reginald Hargrave and Jonathan Leighton, their polished manners at odds with this grimy tavern.

Ethan chuckled, the sound incongruously light in the tense atmosphere. "My good man, surely you're not suggesting that respectable citizens would engage in such nefarious activities?"

The sailor's eyes narrowed. "You'd be surprised what men will do for coin, young master. Even them that's born with silver spoons in their mouths."

Sarah felt Matthew stiffen beside her. She knew he was thinking the same thing she was – they were getting close to something big, something dangerous. She opened her mouth to ask another question, but before she could speak, a heavy hand clamped down on her shoulder.

"I think you have been asking enough questions for one night," a gruff voice growled from behind her.

Sarah turned, her heart pounding, to face a mountain of a man with a face like weathered granite. His small, pig-like eyes glared at them with unmistakable hostility.

The man's meaty hand gripped her shoulder with uncomfortable force, his eyes cold and threatening. She fought to keep her voice steady as she replied, "We meant no harm, sir. Just enjoying a drink and some friendly conversation."

The man's lip curled into a sneer. "Friendly, eh? Sounds more like you're stickin' your noses where they don't belong."

Matthew tensed beside her, his hand inching towards the small knife he kept hidden in his boot. Sarah shot him a warning glance, silently pleading with him not to escalate the situation.

Ethan, ever the picture of composure, smoothly interjected. "My good man, I assure you there's been a misunderstanding.

We're merely tourists, fascinated by the local colour. Perhaps we could buy you a drink to make amends?"

The brute's eyes narrowed, darting between the three of them. Sarah held her breath, praying Ethan's charm would defuse the tension.

After what felt like an eternity, the man grunted and released Sarah's shoulder. "Aye, a drink might smooth things over. But mind you keep your questions to yourselves from now on."

As Ethan signalled the barkeep, Sarah exhaled slowly, her mind whirling. They'd stumbled onto something significant that much was clear. But the danger was palpable now, no longer an abstract concept.

The old sailor who'd been speaking to them earlier had vanished, melting away into the crowd during the confrontation. Sarah scanned the tavern, noting how the other patrons studiously avoided making eye contact.

Matthew leaned in close, his voice barely above a whisper. "We should go. This place isn't safe."

Sarah nodded, her earlier excitement replaced by a gnawing unease. They'd pushed too far, too fast. As Ethan handed a mug to their surly new companion, she caught Matthew's eye and tilted her head towards the door.

THE BROKEN COMPASS & THE SINKING SHIP

※

Sarah and Matthew pushed open the creaky door of The Broken Compass and made their way to the bar, dodging drunken patrons and avoiding eye contact with the more unsavoury characters. Sarah's skin prickled with unease as she felt eyes following their every move.

"What can I get ye?" the bartender growled, eyeing them suspiciously.

"Just looking for some information," Matthew began, but the man's scowl deepened.

"We don't serve that here. Drink or leave."

Matthew opened his mouth to argue, but a familiar voice cut through the din.

"Now, now, my good man. Surely you can spare a moment for some friendly conversation?"

Sarah turned, shocked to see Ethan materialising from the crowd, his refined attire a stark contrast to the tavern's gritty atmosphere. With a charming smile and a flash of coins, he soon had the bartender talking. But despite Ethan's smooth interrogation, they gleaned nothing new about the shipwrecks or smuggling operation.

Frustrated, they left The Broken Compass and made their way to The Sinking Ship. If anything, this tavern was even more disreputable than the last. Sarah's nose wrinkled at the overpowering stench of unwashed bodies and spilled spirits.

They had barely begun questioning the surly patrons when a hulking brute of a man cornered them, his breath reeking of cheap gin.

"You two again," he snarled, recognition flashing in his bloodshot eyes. "Didn't learn your lesson at The Rusty Anchor, did ye?"

Sarah's blood ran cold as she recognised the man who'd threatened them before. She felt Matthew tense beside her, ready for a fight.

But once again, Ethan appeared as if from thin air, placing himself between them and their aggressor.

"Gentlemen, surely we can resolve this amicably," he said smoothly, producing a bottle of fine whiskey from his coat. "Perhaps over a drink?"

Within moments, the man's scowl softened, and he shuffled away, clutching the bottle to his chest like a precious treasure.

"That was... impressive," Sarah breathed, her heart still racing from the close call. She turned to Ethan, gratitude washing over her. "Thank you, Ethan. I don't know what we'd have done without you."

Ethan's smile was warm and reassuring. "Think nothing of it, my dear. I'm just glad I could be of assistance." He glanced around the dingy tavern, his nose wrinkling slightly. "Though I must say, these establishments leave much to be desired. Perhaps we should continue our inquiries in more... reputable quarters?"

Sarah nodded, relieved at the prospect of leaving the foul-smelling tavern behind. It didn't seem like they'd find anything new here either. She turned to Matthew, expecting to see the same relief on his face. Instead, she was taken aback by the cold look he was shooting at Ethan.

"We were managing just fine," Matthew said gruffly, not meeting Ethan's eyes. "No need to go swooping in like some fancy London hero."

Sarah frowned, surprised by Matthew's uncharacteristic rudeness. "Matthew! Ethan's only trying to help. He's been nothing but kind to us."

Matthew's scowl deepened, but he said nothing more. An uncomfortable silence settled over the trio as they made their way out of The Sinking Ship and into the cool night air.

"Well, I must be getting to my papers." Ethan said brightly.

"I'm sure you must." Muttered Matthew.

"Mr Fletcher." Ethan gave Matthew a slight nod that was not returned. "Sarah." Instead of nodding at Sarah, Ethan simply looked deeply into her eyes. Sarah could feel Matthew bristle beside her. "I'll see you soon."

"Goodbye, Ethan." Sarah couldn't help but smile as Ethan strolled off.

"Getting pretty friendly, aren't you?" Matthew remarked.

Sarah opened her mouth to reprimand him, but before she could, Matthew grabbed her quickly and pulled her down behind some crates in the alleyway beside The Sinking Ship.

"Matthew. What are you doing?" Sarah implored, but Matthew just put a finger to his lips.

He whispered. "We've been followed out."

A NARROW ESCAPE

The foul stench of rotting fish and spilled ale assaulted Sarah's nostrils, but she dared not move a muscle. Heavy footsteps echoed off the cobblestones, growing closer with each passing second.

"I swear I saw 'em come this way," a gruff voice growled. "Nosy little rats, asking too many questions."

Sarah's eyes met Matthew's in the dim light. He'd grown up on these streets, knew every nook and cranny of Weymouth's seedier side. If anyone could get them out of this mess, it was Matthew.

The footsteps drew nearer. Sarah held her breath, willing her trembling limbs to stillness. Just when she thought they'd be discovered, Matthew's hand shot out, grabbing a loose cobblestone. In one fluid motion, he hurled it down the alley, where it clattered noisily against a metal dustbin.

"There!" their pursuer shouted, heavy boots pounding away from their hiding spot.

Matthew tugged Sarah's arm. "Now," he whispered urgently. They scrambled to their feet and darted in the opposite direction, weaving through a maze of narrow passageways until they emerged, breathless, near the harbour.

"That was too close," Sarah gasped, leaning against a weathered wooden post to catch her breath. "We need to be more careful."

Matthew nodded grimly. "They're getting bolder. Whatever we're onto, it's big enough that they're willing to risk exposure to stop us."

A few nights later, Sarah stood atop the lighthouse, her gaze sweeping across the moonlit waters. The beam of light cut through the darkness, a steady rhythm that usually brought her comfort. But tonight, unease prickled along her skin.

"Sarah!" Matthew's urgent whisper carried up the spiral staircase. "Come down, quick!"

She hurried down to find Matthew peering out a narrow window, his face tight with worry. "There's someone out there," he murmured, pointing to a shadowy figure lurking near the base of the lighthouse. "Been watching for the past hour."

Sarah's breath caught in her throat. "Do you think they followed us from town?"

Matthew shook his head. "Can't be sure. But we need to be more careful. They're getting closer."

Her eyes strained, trying to make out details in the moonlit darkness.

"We can't just stay here," she whispered, her mind already working on a plan. "If they're watching us, we need to find out why."

Matthew grabbed her arm, his touch gentle but firm. "Sarah, it's too risky. We don't know who's out there or what they're capable of."

She met his gaze, seeing the concern etched in his features. But beneath that worry, she recognised the same determination that burned within her. They'd come too far to back down now.

"We'll be careful," Sarah assured him, her voice low but

steady. "Besides, we have the advantage. We know this lighthouse better than anyone."

Matthew hesitated, then nodded reluctantly. "All right, but we stick together. No heroics."

They crept down the spiral staircase, each step measured and silent. At the base of the lighthouse, they paused, listening intently for any sound from outside.

Sarah reached for the door handle, but Matthew's hand covered hers. "Wait," he breathed, barely audible. He pointed to a thin crack between the door and frame.

Holding her breath, Sarah peered through the gap. The figure had moved closer, now clearly visible in the moonlight. Her eyes widened as she recognized the silhouette – the elegant posture, the fashionable coat.

"It's Ethan," she mouthed to Matthew, confusion and disbelief warring within her. What was he doing here, lurking in the shadows?

Matthew's jaw clenched, his earlier suspicions seeming to solidify. But before either of them could decide on a course of action, Ethan's head snapped up. He looked directly at the lighthouse door, as if sensing their presence.

Ethan took a step towards the lighthouse, his polished shoes crunching softly on the gravel. Sarah held her breath, torn between the urge to fling open the door and demand answers, and the instinct to remain hidden.

"Sarah?" Ethan's voice carried on the night air, smooth as silk despite the late hour. "Are you there? I wanted to make sure you were all right after... well, after the events of the past few days."

Sarah's eyes met Matthew's in the dim light. A muscle twitched in his temple. She could almost hear the unspoken words hanging between them: Don't trust him.

But as she looked back at Ethan, Sarah couldn't help but remember his charm, his worldly knowledge, the way he'd opened her eyes to possibilities beyond Weymouth. Could his presence here truly be sinister?

"I see light," Ethan continued, his tone light but tinged with what sounded like genuine concern. "I do hope I haven't alarmed you by dropping by so late. I just couldn't rest easy without checking on you."

Sarah's hand hovered over the door handle. Matthew's fingers closed around her wrist, a silent plea to wait.

"Ah, well," Ethan sighed after a moment of silence. "Perhaps you're already asleep. I'm glad to see all seems well here. Goodnight, Sarah."

They watched as Ethan turned, his coat swirling dramatically in the sea breeze. He paused, looking back at the lighthouse one last time before striding away, his figure soon swallowed by the darkness.

Sarah let out a shaky breath, her mind whirling. Ethan's words seemed sincere, his concern touching. And yet, the timing, the secrecy of his visit... it all felt off somehow.

"What do you think that was about?" she whispered to Matthew, finally breaking the tense silence.

Matthew's eyes were still fixed on the spot where Ethan had disappeared. "I don't know," he muttered, "but I don't like it one bit."

A LETTER'S TRAIL

"This doesn't make sense," Sarah muttered, tapping a column of figures. "Look here, Matthew. These letters from London – they're all being rerouted through Dorchester before reaching Weymouth."

Matthew leaned in, his shoulder brushing against hers as he examined the ledger. "That's odd. Dorchester's inland. Why would sea-bound messages go there first?"

Sarah's mind raced, piecing together the puzzle. "It's not just London, either. Bristol, Portsmouth... all these coastal cities' communications are taking this strange detour."

She flipped through more pages, her heart quickening as a pattern emerged. "Matthew, look at the dates. Every rerouted message corresponds with a shipwreck or a large shipment we've flagged as suspicious."

Matthew's eyes widened. "Blimey, you're right. But who could orchestrate something like this? It'd take someone with intimate knowledge of the postal system."

Sarah sat back, her gaze falling on the neat signature at the bottom of each ledger. Arthur Finch, Postmaster of Weymouth.

"Mr Finch," she breathed, a chill running down her spine. "It has to be him. He's the only one with the authority to make these changes."

Matthew shook his head in disbelief. "Arthur Finch? But he's been postmaster for years. Everyone in town trusts him."

"Exactly," Sarah said, the pieces falling into place. "Who would suspect dear old Mr Finch? His reputation is spotless."

She stood, pacing the small room as her mind whirled. "Think about it, Matthew. Mr Finch is known for his efficiency, always looking for ways to improve the postal service. What if the smugglers are using that to their advantage?"

Matthew's eyes narrowed. "You mean, they're manipulating him? Making him think these reroutes are for the good of the service?"

Sarah nodded, her heart heavy. "It's brilliant, really. Mr Finch's meticulous nature and sterling reputation provides the perfect cover. He intercepts and reroutes these coded messages, never suspecting he's aiding a criminal enterprise."

"Looks like it's time we meet with Mr Finch." Matthew said. "And see whether he's having the wool pulled over his eyes… Or is a criminal."

∽

THE QUAINT POST OFFICE, with its polished brass fittings and neatly painted sign, seemed an unlikely hub for criminal activity. Yet the evidence they'd uncovered pointed squarely at its occupant.

"Remember," Sarah whispered to Matthew, "we mustn't spook him. Mr Finch might be entirely innocent in all this."

Matthew grinned. "Right. Gentle as a spring breeze, that's us."

They entered, the little bell above the door announcing their arrival. Mr Finch looked up from his desk, his round spectacles perched on the end of his nose.

"Ah, Miss Campbell, Mr Fletcher," he greeted them warmly. "What brings you to my humble establishment today?"

Sarah stepped forward, forcing a smile. "Good afternoon, Mr Finch. We were hoping you might enlighten us about some of the finer points of postal operations. You see, we're working on a... project about efficiency in local businesses."

Arthur Finch's eyes lit up. "Efficiency? Well, you've come to the right place! Pull up a chair, both of you. What would you like to know?"

As they settled in, Sarah exchanged a quick glance with Matthew. Mr Finch's enthusiasm was genuine, his pride in his work evident in every gesture.

"We're particularly interested in mail routes," Matthew began carefully. "How do you determine the best path for a letter to take?"

Mr Finch launched into an explanation, his hands moving animatedly as he spoke of distance calculations and transport schedules. Sarah listened intently, her heart sinking as she realised just how deeply the smugglers might have exploited this good man's dedication.

"And what about rerouting?" Sarah asked, her voice soft. "We've noticed some letters from coastal cities seem to go through Dorchester before reaching Weymouth. Is there a reason for that?"

A flicker of confusion passed over Mr Finch's face. "Dorchester? That's odd. I don't recall implementing any such change." He rifled through some papers on his desk. "Although... there was a directive from the regional office about optimising certain routes. Let me see..."

Sarah leaned forward, her voice gentle. "Mr Finch, we believe someone may be using your system for... nefarious purposes."

Arthur Finch's head snapped up, his eyes wide behind his spectacles. "What? That's impossible. I run a tight ship here, I assure you."

"We know you do," Matthew said soothingly. "That's why we've come to you. We think someone might be taking advantage of your efficiency and good reputation."

Sarah watched as the colour drained from Mr Finch's face. His grey eyes, usually sharp and observant, now brimmed with a mixture of shock and distress. The postmaster's hands trembled slightly as he lowered the papers he'd been holding.

"Good heavens," he whispered, his voice barely audible. "How could I have been so blind?"

Sarah's heart ached for the man. She'd known Mr Finch since childhood, had seen him diligently sorting letters and packages day after day. The thought that his dedication had been twisted for such nefarious purposes seemed cruel beyond measure.

"It's not your fault, Mr Finch," she said gently. "These people, they're clever. They've fooled a lot of good folk."

Arthur Finch removed his spectacles, pinching the bridge of his nose. When he looked up, his eyes were filled with a deep, sorrowful remorse. "But I should have noticed. All those redirected letters, the unusual patterns... I prided myself on efficiency, and instead, I've been aiding criminals."

Matthew leant forward. "You can help us put a stop to it, Mr Finch. Your knowledge of the postal system could be invaluable."

The postmaster straightened in his chair, a spark of determination replacing the shock in his eyes. "Yes, of course. Anything I can do to make this right." He stood up, moving with purpose towards a locked cabinet. "I'll give you full access to our records. Every letter, every package, every route change. We'll get to the bottom of this, I swear it."

Sarah felt a surge of hope as she watched Mr Finch unlock

the cabinet, his hands now steady with resolve. She caught Matthew's eye, seeing her own mix of relief and determination mirrored there. With Arthur Finch's help, they were one step closer to unravelling the mystery.

REVELATIONS IN LETTERS

Sarah leaned over the desk, concentrating as she studied the intercepted messages spread before her. Mr Finch hovered nearby, his spectacles perched on the end of his nose as he offered insights into the postal codes and routing numbers scrawled across the papers.

"Look here," Sarah said, tapping a finger on a particular line. "This shipment was marked for Dorchester, but the actual destination seems to be a cove just east of Weymouth."

Matthew nodded, his eyes scanning the document. "And the sender's name... it's an alias. 'J. Smith' - how original," he scoffed.

Mr Finch cleared his throat. "I've noticed that name recurring quite frequently in recent months. Always with peculiar routing instructions."

As they delved deeper into the messages, a pattern began to emerge. Sarah's heart raced with each new discovery, the pieces of the puzzle slowly clicking into place. The network was vast, stretching far beyond Weymouth's borders, with tentacles reaching into the highest echelons of society.

"These aren't just simple smugglers," Sarah murmured, her voice tinged with awe and dread. "This is organised, sophisticated. Look at how they've coordinated these shipments with the tides and lighthouse schedules."

Matthew's jaw clenched. "They've been right under our noses this whole time. Using our own systems against us."

As the afternoon wore on, Sarah's mind whirled with the implications of their discoveries. Names began to surface – some familiar, others shrouded in mystery. Each decoded message brought them tantalisingly closer to the truth, yet raised a host of new questions.

Sarah's thoughts drifted momentarily to Ethan. His charming smile and tales of London society seemed a world away from the gritty reality of their investigation. Yet she couldn't shake the feeling that he somehow fit into this puzzle.

A TENSE ENCOUNTER

⚜

Sarah's satchel was heavy with the weight of their discoveries. Matthew walked beside her, his usual easy stride now tense and measured. The late afternoon sun cast long shadows across the cobblestones.

"We should head back to the lighthouse," Matthew said, his voice gruff. "Go over everything we've learned."

Sarah nodded, but her eyes were drawn to a familiar figure approaching from the direction of the Esplanade. Ethan, resplendent in a tailored suit, tipped his hat as he neared.

"Sarah, Mr Fletcher," Ethan greeted them, his smile warm. "What a pleasant surprise. I was just on my way to the Pavilion for tea. Would you care to join me?"

Sarah felt torn between the allure of Ethan's sophistication and the pressing need to continue their investigation. She glanced at Matthew.

"That's very kind, Mr Blackwood," Sarah began, "but we—"

"We have urgent business to attend to," Matthew cut in, his tone brusque. "Another time, perhaps."

Ethan raised an eyebrow, his gaze moving between them. "Of course, I wouldn't want to intrude on your... affairs." He turned to Sarah, his voice softening. "Perhaps we could arrange a convenient time for that tour of the lighthouse you promised, Miss Campbell?"

Before Sarah could respond, Matthew stepped forward, placing himself slightly between her and Ethan. "Sarah's been quite busy with her duties. I'm not sure when she'll have the time for social calls."

Sarah felt a flare of irritation at Matthew's presumption. "I'm sure I can find a moment, Ethan," she said, offering Ethan a smile. "I'll send word when I'm available."

As Ethan bid them farewell and continued on his way, Sarah turned to Matthew, her eyes narrowing. "What was that about? Since when do you decide my schedule?"

Matthew's face flushed, but his expression remained stubborn. "I don't trust him, Sarah. There's something off about the way he always seems to turn up at the most 'convenient' times."

"Or perhaps he's just being friendly," Sarah retorted, her voice rising slightly. "Not everyone has ulterior motives, Matthew."

As they made their way back to the lighthouse the tension between them was palpable, but she pushed her frustration aside, knowing they had more important matters to focus on.

Once inside, Sarah spread out the documents they'd gathered onto the worn wooden table. Matthew stood beside her, his presence both comforting and irritating in equal measure.

"We need to cross-reference these shipping manifests with the postal records Mr Finch provided," Sarah said, her voice steady despite her inner turmoil.

Matthew nodded, pulling up a chair. "I'll start with the dates we know for certain. You take the names we've identified."

They worked in silence for a while, the only sound the rustling of papers and the occasional scratch of a pencil. Sarah found herself stealing glances at Matthew, noting the furrow of concentration on his brow.

"Look at this," Matthew said suddenly, pushing a document towards her. "There's a pattern in the routing instructions. Every third Tuesday, a package is redirected through Dorchester."

Sarah leaned in, her shoulder brushing against Matthew's. She ignored the flutter in her stomach at the contact. "You're right. And look here – the sender's name changes, but the handwriting is the same."

Their eyes met, a spark of shared excitement momentarily eclipsing their earlier disagreement.

"We should show this to Mr Finch," Sarah said. "He might be able to identify the handwriting."

Matthew nodded, a hint of a smile on his face. "Good thinking. We can head to the post office first thing tomorrow."

As they continued to work, the familiar rhythm of their partnership reasserted itself.

"Sarah," Matthew said softly, breaking the silence. "I'm sorry about earlier. With Ethan, I mean. I shouldn't have spoken for you."

Sarah looked up, meeting his earnest gaze. She felt a wave of affection for her oldest friend, mixed with a lingering frustration she couldn't quite shake.

"I appreciate that, Matthew," she replied. "But I need you to trust my judgment. We're in this together, remember?"

Matthew nodded, his expression a mix of relief and something else Sarah couldn't quite decipher. "Together," he agreed, turning back to the documents before them.

UNSEEN EYES

Skirts rustling against the rough stone walls, Sarah hurried down the narrow alley. She glanced over her shoulder, catching a glimpse of Matthew close behind. The sound of footsteps echoed off the buildings, but Sarah couldn't tell if they belonged to her and Matthew or to their unseen pursuer.

They emerged onto the moonlit street, both breathing heavily. Sarah's eyes darted around, searching for any sign of danger. The town seemed unnaturally quiet, the usual sounds of the harbour muffled by the fog rolling in from the sea.

"Do you think we lost them?" Sarah whispered.

Matthew shook his head, his expression grim. "I'm not sure. But we can't take any chances. We need to get somewhere safe."

As they made their way towards the lighthouse, Sarah couldn't shake the feeling of being watched. Every shadow seemed to hide a threat, every unexpected sound made her jump. She thought back to the series of strange occurrences over the past week – the mysterious letter warning them to "mind their own business," the loose wheel on Matthew's cart that nearly caused an accident, the sudden illness that struck Mr

Finch just as he was about to share crucial information with them.

"Matthew," Sarah said softly as they approached the lighthouse, "I think we're getting close to something big. These aren't just coincidences anymore."

Matthew nodded, his jaw set with determination. "I know. But we can't stop now, Sarah. Too many lives are at stake."

As they reached the lighthouse door, Sarah caught movement out of the corner of her eye. She turned sharply. There, half-hidden in the shadows across the street, stood a tall figure in a dark coat. The same figure she'd glimpsed outside the tavern, and again near the post office.

"Matthew," she hissed, gripping his arm. "Look."

Matthew followed her gaze, his body tensing beside her. For a long moment, they stood frozen, staring at the shadowy figure. Then, as suddenly as it had appeared, it melted back into the darkness.

Sarah's hand trembled as she fumbled with the lighthouse key. Once inside, she leaned against the door, her heart pounding. "They're watching us, Matthew. They know what we're doing."

Matthew's face was a mix of concern and resolve. "Then we must be on the right track. We can't back down now, Sarah. We're too close to the truth."

Sarah took a deep breath, steadying herself. "It's like trying to piece together a puzzle with half the pieces missing," she murmured.

The rhythmic sweep of the lighthouse beam cast alternating light and shadow across the room, mirroring the ebb and flow of Sarah's thoughts. She turned to gaze out at the vast expanse of the sea, its dark waters concealing countless secrets.

"Do you ever wonder if we're in over our heads?" Sarah asked, her voice tinged with a hint of doubt.

Matthew came to stand beside her. "Every day," he admitted.

"But then I think about all the lives at stake, all the families torn apart by these shipwrecks. We can't give up, Sarah."

Sarah nodded, drawing strength from his words and the steady rotation of the lighthouse beam. Its unwavering light cut through the darkness, a beacon of hope for ships lost at sea.

"You're right," she said. "We've come too far to back down now. Whatever it takes, we'll see this through to the end."

Together, they bent over the documents once more, the lighthouse beam sweeping methodically across the dark waters.

THE LURE OF TRUTH

⚜

Sarah clutched the crumpled note in her hand. The anonymous tip had arrived that morning, slipped under the lighthouse door. Its contents burned in her mind: Jonathan Leighton, a respected figure in Weymouth, implicated in the very smuggling ring they'd been investigating for months.

"A meeting at Nothe Fort," she murmured, her eyes scanning the horizon where the fort's silhouette loomed against the darkening sky.

Matthew paced the lighthouse floor, his brow furrowed with concern. "It could be a trap, Sarah. We don't know who sent this information or why."

Sarah knew he was right to be cautious, but the prospect of finally uncovering concrete evidence was too tempting to ignore. She'd seen the pain in the eyes of families torn apart by the shipwrecks, heard the whispers of fear in the streets of Weymouth. They needed answers, and this might be their best chance.

"We can't let this opportunity slip away," Sarah said, her voice steady despite the flutter of nerves in her stomach. "If Leighton is involved, we need to know."

"Sarah, please," Matthew implored, his eyes filled with worry. "We can't rush into this. It's too dangerous."

She knew he was right. The risks were undeniable, and they'd already had too many close calls. Sarah looked down at the note again, her fingers tracing the hastily scrawled words.

"You're right," she conceded with a sigh. "We need to be smart about this. Going to Nothe Fort alone would be foolish."

Matthew's shoulders visibly relaxed. He stepped closer, placing a gentle hand on her arm. "We'll figure this out together, Sarah. Just like we always do."

Sarah nodded, managing a small smile. "Thank you, Matthew. For looking out for me."

As the sun dipped below the horizon, Matthew bid her goodnight and headed home. Sarah watched from the lighthouse window as his figure disappeared into the gathering darkness. She waited, counting the minutes, her resolve strengthening with each passing moment.

Once she was certain Matthew was far enough away, Sarah grabbed her cloak and a small lantern. Her heart raced as she quietly slipped out of the lighthouse and into the night. The path to Nothe Fort stretched before her, shrouded in shadows.

"I'm sorry, Matthew," she whispered to the empty air. "But I have to do this."

With determined steps, Sarah set out towards the looming silhouette of Nothe Fort.

WHISPERS IN THE WALLS

The ancient structure of Nothe Fort loomed before Sarah, its moss-covered walls a testament to centuries of silent vigilance. Twilight had settled over Weymouth, casting long shadows that seemed to reach out like grasping fingers.

She paused at the base of the fort, her eyes scanning the weathered stone for any sign of movement. The air hung heavy with the scent of brine and decay. Sarah pulled her cloak tighter around her shoulders, suppressing a shiver that had nothing to do with the evening chill.

As she stood there, the eerie silence pressed in around her. It was broken only by the occasional mournful cry of a seabird wheeling overhead and the distant, rhythmic murmur of waves crashing against the cliffs far below. The sounds seemed to emphasise the isolation of her position.

She took a deep breath, steeling herself for what lay ahead. The anonymous note crinkled in her pocket. Jonathan Leighton's potential involvement in the smuggling ring could be the key to unravelling the entire conspiracy. The thought of finally bringing justice to those who'd suffered from the shipwrecks gave her courage.

Sarah raised her lantern, its feeble light barely penetrating the gloom that cloaked the fort's entrance. She took a tentative step forward, her free hand brushing against the cold stone wall for guidance. The fort seemed to hold its breath, waiting.

She stepped into the fort's yawning entrance. The air inside was stale and heavy, thick with the weight of centuries. Her lantern cast dancing shadows on the walls, transforming innocuous shapes into menacing spectres.

She moved cautiously, each footfall echoing in the oppressive silence. The narrow staircases twisted upward, their worn steps a testament to countless feet that had trod this path before. Sarah's free hand trailed along the damp stone walls, steadying herself as she climbed.

The winding corridors seemed to shift and change with each turn. Sarah fought back a rising sense of disorientation, focusing on her goal. She needed to find a vantage point, somewhere she could observe without being seen.

As she ascended, Sarah's mind raced. What if Jonathan Leighton was here now? What secrets might she uncover? The thought both thrilled and terrified her.

At last, she reached a high chamber. Moonlight filtered through a narrow window, mingling with the warm glow of her lantern. Sarah extinguished the flame, allowing her eyes to adjust to the darkness.

She crept towards the window, staying low. From this perch, she could see much of the fort's interior courtyard spread out below. Sarah pressed herself against the wall, melting into the shadows.

Her breath caught as she spotted movement in the courtyard. Two figures emerged from a doorway, their hushed voices barely carrying on the night air. Sarah strained to make out their features, her heart racing. Could one of them be Jonathan Leighton?

PROTECTIVE INSTINCTS

Matthew Fletcher couldn't shake the gnawing unease in his gut. Sarah had gone to Nothe Fort alone, despite his protests. He clenched his fists, frustrated by her stubbornness. Yet, a part of him couldn't help but admire her resilience and determination. It was one of the things that had drawn him to her in the first place.

He paced the docks, the salty air doing nothing to calm his nerves. The thought of Sarah facing unknown dangers alone ate at him. Against his better judgment, Matthew found himself moving towards the fort, driven by a feeling he couldn't quite name.

The night air was thick with fog as Matthew made his way along the darkened path to Nothe Fort. His footsteps were quick but cautious, his sea-trained eyes scanning the surroundings for any sign of Sarah or potential threats. The fort loomed before him, its stone walls seeming to absorb what little moonlight filtered through the clouds.

Worry ate at Matthew, but determination propelled him forward. His protective instincts, honed by years of facing the unpredictable sea, were in full force. He'd faced storms and treacherous waters, but nothing had prepared him for the fear he felt now – the fear of losing Sarah.

As he approached the fort's entrance, Matthew paused, listening intently for any sound that might betray Sarah's presence or danger. The only noise was the distant crash of waves against the shore and his own ragged breathing.

PERIL AT NOTHE FORT

*S*arah inched closer to the edge of the fort's wall. The salty sea air whipped at her face, carrying with it the faint murmur of voices. She strained her ears, desperate to catch every word.

"The next shipment needs to be larger," a gruff voice said. Sarah recognised it immediately as Jonathan Leighton's. "We can't afford any more mishaps."

She peered over the ledge, careful to keep herself hidden in the shadows. Below, a group of men huddled together, their faces obscured by the darkness. But there was no mistaking Leighton's broad shoulders and commanding presence.

"What about the lighthouse keeper?" another voice asked. "He's been asking questions."

Sarah's breath caught in her throat. They were talking about Mr Thorne.

"Leave him to me," Leighton growled. "We've got bigger problems. The Harbourmaster's starting to suspect something."

Sarah's mind raced, trying to memorise every detail. Names, dates, locations – each piece of information could be crucial to unravelling the smuggling operation.

"We'll need to move the drop point," a third voice chimed in. "The caves near Durdle Door should work."

"Good," Leighton nodded. "And make sure the next wreck looks convincing. We can't have anyone suspecting foul play."

Sarah's blood ran cold. They were planning another shipwreck. How many innocent lives would be put at risk for their greed?

She leaned forward, straining to hear more. But as she did, a loose stone shifted beneath her foot. Sarah froze, her heart stopping as the pebble clattered down the fort's wall.

"What was that?" One of the voices exclaimed, and they all went quiet.

Sarah held her breath, and hoped the thunder that was her heartbeat wouldn't give her away.

After what was an agonisingly long time, Leighton said "Must have just been one of those gulls. What were you saying?"

Sarah let out a sigh of relief, but the moment of respite was short lived.

Suddenly, she felt a sudden, ominous presence behind her. The hairs on the back of her neck stood on end, but before she could turn to face the threat, a powerful force slammed into her back. She lurched forward, her stomach dropping as she teetered on the edge of the fort's wall.

Time seemed to slow as Sarah's body pitched over the precipice. In that moment of terror, her survival instincts kicked in. Her hands shot out, desperately grasping at the rough stone surface. Her fingers found purchase, scraping against the moss-covered rocks as she clung to the edge with all her might.

The wind howled around her, drowning out the panicked gasps that escaped her lips. Sarah's arms trembled with the effort of holding on, her feet scrabbling against the wall for any kind of foothold. The jagged stones bit into her skin, drawing blood, but she barely noticed the pain. All that mattered was not falling.

"Help!" Sarah tried to cry out, but her voice came out as little more than a choked whisper. She could hear the men below, their voices rising in alarm. Had they spotted her? Or had her attacker alerted them?

Sarah's mind raced, torn between the immediate danger of her precarious position and the implications of what she'd overheard. Mr Thorne was in danger. Another shipwreck was being planned. And now, someone had tried to silence her permanently.

She gritted her teeth, forcing herself to focus. She couldn't let go. She couldn't fall. Too many lives depended on what she knew.

With a herculean effort, Sarah began to pull herself up, inch by agonising inch. Her muscles screamed in protest, but she refused to give in. She had to survive. She had to warn Matthew, Mr Thorne, and the others. She prayed to the Lord to give her the strength.

As she struggled, Sarah became aware of rapid footsteps approaching from behind. Friend or foe, she couldn't be sure. But in her current position, she was utterly vulnerable.

She could hear the men below, their voices rising in alarm, but she couldn't make out their words over the roaring in her head.

Just as her strength began to fail, a familiar voice cut through the chaos.

"Sarah!"

Matthew's panicked cry sent a jolt of hope through her. She wanted to call back, to let him know she was there, but fear had stolen her voice.

A strong hand grasped her arm. Sarah was pulled upward, away from the dizzying drop. With a final, desperate heave, she tumbled forward onto solid ground, colliding with Matthew as they both fell in a tangle of limbs.

For a moment, they lay there, gasping for breath. Sarah's

entire body trembled, the adrenaline still coursing through her veins. She could feel Matthew's rapid heartbeat where his chest pressed against her back, his arms still wrapped protectively around her.

"Sarah," Matthew panted, his voice thick with relief and fear. "What were you thinking?"

She tried to respond, but her words came out as a choked sob. The reality of how close she'd come to death crashed over her. Sarah turned, burying her face in Matthew's shoulder as she shook with silent tears.

Matthew held her tightly, one hand gently stroking her hair. "It's all right," he murmured. "You're safe now. I've got you."

As her panic began to subside, Sarah became aware of a faint sound – retreating footsteps. She lifted her head, peering into the darkness, but saw no sign of her attacker.

The cool stone beneath them contrasted sharply with the warmth of Matthew's embrace.

Slowly, they pulled themselves into a sitting position, still clinging to one another. Sarah's tear-stained cheeks glistened in the dim light. Their eyes met, and Sarah felt a jolt of electricity course through her. Matthew's gaze was filled with concern, relief, and something else – an intensity she'd never seen before.

"I thought I'd lost you," Matthew whispered, his voice hoarse with emotion. His hand cupped her face gently, thumb brushing away a stray tear.

Sarah leaned into his touch. "You saved me," she breathed.

They sat there, faces mere inches apart. Sarah's gaze flickered to Matthew's lips, then back to his eyes. She saw her own longing reflected there, a depth of feeling that both thrilled and terrified her.

Their faces were so close she could feel his warm breath on her skin.

The sound of approaching footsteps echoed through the

fort. Sarah and Matthew jerked apart, the spell broken. They scrambled to their feet, faces flushed and breathing heavy.

Lantern light danced across the ancient stones as a group rounded the corner. Sarah blinked against the sudden brightness, her eyes widening as she recognised the figure at the front of the search party.

"Sarah! Thank Heavens you're all right," Ethan called out, his voice laced with concern. He rushed forward, his polished boots clicking against the stone floor.

Sarah felt Matthew stiffen beside her, his hand instinctively reaching for hers. She gave it a quick squeeze before dropping it, acutely aware of the others' presence.

"We've been searching everywhere for you," Ethan continued, his eyes roaming over Sarah as if checking for injuries. "When you didn't return to the lighthouse, Mr Thorne raised the alarm."

Sarah opened her mouth to respond, but the words caught in her throat. How could she explain what had happened without revealing what she'd overheard? Her mind raced, trying to formulate a plausible story.

"It was my fault," Matthew stepped in, his voice steady despite the tension Sarah could feel radiating from him. "I... I asked Sarah to meet me here. We lost track of time."

Ethan's gaze shifted between them, his brow furrowing slightly. "At this hour? In such a dangerous location?"

Ethan's piercing gaze flickered between Sarah and Matthew. His expression remained unreadable, a mask of polite concern that revealed nothing of his true thoughts. She swallowed hard, praying he wouldn't press further.

"Well," Ethan said at last, his voice smooth as silk, "I'm just relieved you're both safe. These old fortifications can be treacherous, especially at night."

Sarah nodded, not trusting herself to speak.

GUARDED SECRETS

※

The journey back to the lighthouse was a blur of hushed voices and furtive glances. Sarah's mind whirled with the night's events, her body still trembling from the near-death experience. She longed to confide in Matthew, to share what she'd overheard, but Ethan's watchful eyes made it impossible.

As they approached the lighthouse, Sarah spotted Mr Thorne's silhouette in the doorway. His weathered face was etched with worry, his grey eyes scanning the group until they landed on her. Relief washed over his features, and Sarah felt a pang of guilt for causing him such distress.

"Sarah, my girl," Mr Thorne breathed, pulling her into a fierce embrace. "Thank the Lord you're all right."

Once inside the familiar confines of the lighthouse, Sarah felt some of the tension leave her body. She sank into a chair, Matthew taking the seat beside her. Mr Thorne bustled about, preparing tea with shaking hands while Ethan leaned against the wall, his keen gaze never leaving Sarah.

"Now," Mr Thorne said, setting steaming cups before them, "what in Heaven's name happened out there?"

Sarah's eyes met Matthew's. In that silent exchange, they reached an understanding. They couldn't reveal everything, not with Ethan present, but they had to give some explanation for their reckless behaviour.

"We were at Nothe Fort," Sarah began, her voice steadier than she felt. "We thought we saw something suspicious and went to investigate."

Matthew nodded, picking up the thread. "It was foolish, we know. But we've been hearing rumours about smuggling operations, and we thought we might uncover something."

Sarah met Matthew's gaze, silently communicating their shared secret. She turned back to Mr Thorne and Ethan, her fingers nervously twisting the fabric of her skirt.

"We didn't mean to cause any alarm," she said. "We just wanted to help uncover the truth about what's been happening to the ships."

Mr Thorne's brow furrowed. "Sarah, my girl, I understand your intentions, but you can't go putting yourself in danger like that. The fort is no place for young people to be wandering about at night."

Sarah nodded, guilt washing over her. She hated lying to Mr Thorne, but she couldn't risk revealing what she'd overheard. Not yet. Not with Ethan in the room.

"It won't happen again, sir," Matthew added, his voice steady despite the tension Sarah could feel radiating from him. "We should have known better."

Ethan pushed himself off the wall, his polished boots clicking against the floor as he approached. "Well, I'm just glad you're both safe," he said, his smile not quite reaching his eyes. "Though I must say, I'm curious about these smuggling rumours. Perhaps you could enlighten us?"

Sarah knew they were treading on dangerous ground. How much could they reveal without putting themselves at risk?

"It's nothing concrete," Sarah said carefully, forcing her voice to remain steady. "Just whispers we've heard around town. People talking about strange lights at sea, ships veering off course for no reason. We thought there might be something to it, but..." She trailed off, shrugging helplessly.

Ethan's gaze bore into her, and Sarah felt as though he could see right through her flimsy explanation. But after a moment, he nodded, his charming smile back in place. "Well, it's admirable that you want to help the town. But perhaps leave the investigating to the proper authorities, hmm?"

Sarah nodded, relief flooding through her. She glanced at Matthew, seeing her own mixture of fear and determination reflected in his eyes. They had escaped detection for now, but they both knew this was far from over.

∽

Sarah paced the lighthouse's circular room, her nerves frayed as she waited for Ethan and Matthew to depart. What she'd witnessed at Nothe Fort pressed upon her, demanding to be shared. As the door closed behind the two young men, Sarah turned to Mr Thorne, her heart pounding.

"There's more," she blurted out, her voice trembling. "So much more than what I said earlier."

Mr Thorne's weathered face creased with concern. "What is it, my girl?"

Sarah steadied herself against the cool stone wall. "I overheard a meeting at the fort. Jonathan Leighton was there, discussing smuggling operations and planned shipwrecks."

Mr Thorne's eyes widened, but he remained silent, allowing Sarah to continue.

"And... they mentioned you by name, Mr Thorne. They said if you became a problem, they'd... they'd make sure you had an accident."

Mr Thorne sank into a nearby chair, his hands gripping the armrests. "Good Heavens," he muttered.

Sarah knelt beside him, her eyes brimming with tears. "I'm so sorry, Mr Thorne. I never meant to put you in danger."

Mr Thorne patted her hand, his touch reassuring despite the gravity of the situation. "You've done right by telling me, Sarah. We'll need to be cautious from here on out."

He stood, pacing the room as Sarah had done moments before. "I think it's time we brought on another assistant here at the lighthouse. Someone to help with the workload, yes, but also... for security."

Sarah nodded, relief washing over her at Mr Thorne's calm acceptance of her words. "Do you have someone in mind?"

"I do," Mr Thorne said, his voice firm with resolve. "An old navy friend of mine. He'll be discreet, and he knows how to handle himself in a tight spot."

ALEXANDER DAVIES

Sarah hadn't expected the new assistant to arrive so soon. The man's broad shoulders and steady gait spoke of strength. Mr Thorne greeted the newcomer at the door, his voice carrying up to where Sarah stood.

"Alexander, my old friend! Welcome to South Point."

Sarah descended the spiral staircase. As she reached the bottom, she caught her first proper glimpse of Alexander Davies. He was a man of few words, it seemed, offering only a nod in response to Mr Thorne's warm welcome.

"Sarah, come meet our new assistant," Mr Thorne beckoned.

She stepped forward, extending her hand. "Pleased to meet you, Mr Davies."

Alexander's grip was firm but gentle. "Miss Campbell," His voice was gravelly, but with a hint of a sing-song nature to it. A slight Irish accent danced across his words.

In the days that followed, Sarah found that Alexander slipped into life at the lighthouse with surprising ease. He was a quiet presence, moving about his duties with efficiency and purpose. Sarah often caught sight of him carrying heavy loads of supplies or tending to maintenance tasks that had long been neglected.

Despite his reticence, Sarah couldn't help but feel grateful for Alexander's presence. There was something reassuring about having another pair of capable hands around, especially given the dangers they now knew lurked in the shadows of Weymouth.

On his first evening at South Point, as Sarah climbed the lighthouse steps to begin her watch, she passed Alexander on his way down. He paused, stepping aside to let her pass.

"All's quiet, Miss Campbell," he said, his eyes scanning the horizon beyond the window. "But I'll be nearby if you need anything."

Sarah nodded, a small smile tugging at her lips. "Thank you, Mr Davies."

As she took her place by the great Fresnel lens, a sense of calm settled over her. The familiar routines continued, but now with an added layer of security. Alexander Davies may have been a man of few words, but his steady presence spoke volumes.

THE WEB TIGHTENS

◈

Sarah's eyes strained in the flickering lamplight as she hunched over the scattered papers on the lighthouse's worn wooden table. Matthew sat beside her, his brow furrowed in concentration, while Arthur nervously adjusted his spectacles across from them. The night air hung heavy with the severity of their discoveries.

"Look at this," Sarah whispered, sliding a crumpled letter towards Matthew. "It's the same handwriting as the note we found in 'Lady Isabel's' logbook."

Matthew nodded grimly. "And here's another mention of 'The Pelican.' That's got to be their code name for Jonathan Leighton."

Arthur cleared his throat. "I-I never imagined... All those redirected letters. I thought I was improving the postal service, not aiding criminals."

Sarah placed a reassuring hand on the postmaster's arm. "You couldn't have known, Mr Finch. But your help now is invaluable."

As they delved deeper into the pile of intercepted messages, a pattern began to emerge. Coded references to shipments, coordinates that matched the locations of recent wrecks, and fragments of names that hinted at the involvement of Weymouth's elite.

"Good Heavens," Matthew muttered.

"We can't trust anyone," Sarah said, a chill running down her spine despite the warmth of the lighthouse. "Who knows how deep this conspiracy runs?"

Arthur nodded solemnly. "It's not just smuggling anymore, is it? These wrecks, the lives lost – it's murder."

The gravity of their discovery settled over the room like a heavy fog. Sarah met Matthew's eyes, seeing her own determination reflected there.

"We have to stop them," Sarah said, her voice steady despite the fear coiling in her stomach. "No matter the cost."

THE WEIGHT OF THE SEA

The setting sun painted the sky in hues of orange and pink, casting a warm glow over the promenade. Ethan's presence beside Sarah felt both exhilarating and comforting, a stark contrast to the tension that had consumed her thoughts lately.

"You look radiant this evening, Sarah," Ethan said, his voice smooth as silk. "The sea air certainly agrees with you."

Sarah suppressed a blush. "Thank you, Ethan. I must admit, these outings are a welcome distraction from my duties."

Ethan's eyes sparkled with interest. "Ah, yes. Your work at the lighthouse. I find it fascinating, truly. Next week, there's to be a performance of Shakespeare at the Pavilion. Would you do me the honour of accompanying me?"

Sarah's eyes widened with excitement. "Shakespeare? Oh, Ethan, I'd be delighted!"

The following week, Sarah sat beside Ethan in the plush velvet seats of the Weymouth Pavilion. The theatre buzzed with anticipation as the curtain rose. Sarah watched, transfixed, as the actors brought the Bard's words to life. During the intermission, Ethan introduced her to several well-dressed patrons, his hand resting lightly on the small of her back as he guided her through the social niceties.

With each outing, Sarah felt her world expanding. Ethan took her to lectures on the latest scientific discoveries, introduced her to new forms of art, and shared stories of his travels abroad. She found herself eagerly anticipating their time together, her mind whirling with new ideas and possibilities.

One afternoon, as they shared tea at a quaint café overlooking the harbour, Ethan leaned in close. "You know, Sarah, and of course you know because I say it all the time. But I truly do believe you have the potential to make quite a splash in London society. Your quick wit and natural charm would open many doors for you there."

Sarah felt foolish for ever suspecting Ethan could be a part of the nefarious conspiracy that she and Matthew had been uncovering. How could someone with such grace, such class, ever be involved in something like that?

∽

MATTHEW STOOD ON THE DOCK, his hands calloused from a long day of fishing, watching as Sarah and Ethan strolled arm-in-arm along the Esplanade. The sight twisted his gut, a mix of jealousy and worry churning inside him. He couldn't help but notice how Sarah's face lit up when Ethan spoke, how she laughed at his jokes and hung on his every word.

"Quite the pair, aren't they?" Old Tom, a fellow fisherman, remarked beside him.

Matthew grunted in response. He couldn't shake the feeling that there was more to Ethan than met the eye. The man's charm seemed too polished, his stories too convenient.

"Sarah deserves better," Matthew muttered, more to himself than to Tom.

As he watched them disappear around a corner, Matthew

felt a pang of inadequacy. What could he offer Sarah compared to Ethan's wealth and sophistication? His world was one of early mornings, rough seas, and the smell of fish. Ethan's was one of grand parties, fine clothes, and exciting adventures in London.

Over the next few weeks, Matthew threw himself into his work with renewed vigour. He spent longer hours at sea, pushing his boat further out in search of better catches. When he wasn't fishing, he pored over the documents they'd gathered about the smuggling ring, determined to crack the case wide open.

Sarah noticed the change in Matthew's behaviour. She'd stop by the docks, hoping to catch him between trips, but he always seemed to be just leaving or too busy mending nets.

"Matthew," she called out one afternoon, spotting him loading his boat. "I haven't seen you in ages. Is everything all right?"

He paused, not meeting her eyes. "Just busy, Sarah. You know how it is."

Sarah frowned, sensing the distance between them. She opened her mouth to say more, but Matthew cut her off.

"I've got to get going. The tide waits for no one."

As he pushed off from the dock, Sarah stood watching, her brow furrowed in confusion and concern. She couldn't shake the feeling that she was losing her oldest friend, but she didn't know how to bridge the growing gap between them.

BREAKING THE CODE

"Look here," Sarah whispered, her finger tracing a line of text. "This shipping manifest matches perfectly with the coded message we intercepted last week."

Matthew nodded, a glimmer of excitement in his eyes. It was one of the increasingly rare occasions when he wasn't too busy to sit and search with her. "And the signature at the bottom - it's Beatrice Wentworth's."

Sarah's heart raced as the pieces began to fall into place. They had suspected Beatrice's involvement for weeks, but this was the first concrete evidence linking her to the smuggling operation.

"And here," Matthew continued, sliding another document forward. "Jonathan Leighton's name appears in three separate coded communications. Always in connection with shipment schedules."

Sarah's mind whirled as she connected the dots. "The tea room, the ship brokerage... they're all fronts for their illegal activities."

As they pored over the evidence, a disturbing pattern

emerged. Sarah's hand trembled slightly as she placed a final document on top of the pile.

"Edward Collins," she said. "The parish priest. His name is here too, buried in the coded messages."

Matthew's jaw clenched. "Using his position to gather information and divert suspicion. Clever, but despicable."

Sarah nodded, a mix of triumph and unease settling in her stomach. They had cracked the code, uncovering a web of deceit that stretched far beyond what they had initially imagined.

"We need to document everything," Sarah said, reaching for a fresh sheet of paper. "Every meeting, every shipment, every communication. We can't leave any room for doubt."

As the night wore on, Sarah and Matthew meticulously compiled their evidence. Photographs were carefully labelled, notes were cross-referenced, and witness testimonies were recorded in detail.

By the time the first rays of dawn began to peek through the lighthouse windows, they had assembled a substantial case against the prominent citizens involved in the smuggling ring.

Sarah leaned back in her chair, exhaustion and exhilaration warring within her. "We've done it, Matthew. We've finally uncovered the truth."

Matthew nodded, but his expression remained serious. "We have, but we can't move yet. There's still something missing."

"What do you mean?" Sarah asked, frowning.

"We've identified the key players, but we still don't know who's pulling all the strings. Who's the mastermind behind it all?"

Sarah's eyes widened as she realised the truth in Matthew's words. "You're right. We need to find the root of this corruption, not just cut off the branches."

Sᴀʀᴀʜ's ᴇʏᴇs widened as she deciphered the latest coded message. Her heart raced, and she motioned urgently for Matthew and Arthur to join her at the small desk in the lighthouse's lantern room.

"Look at this," she whispered, her finger tracing the carefully disguised words. "It's a shipment. A big one."

Matthew leaned in, his brow furrowed in concentration. "When?"

"Two months from now," Sarah replied, her voice tight with excitement and apprehension. "And it involves all of them – Wentworth, Leighton, Collins. Even names we haven't seen before."

"That's when the Regatta is!" Matthew exclaimed. "Biggest sporting event of the year. Who knows how many boats will be in the harbour!"

Arthur adjusted his spectacles, peering at the message. "Good heavens," he murmured. "This could be our chance to expose the entire operation."

Sarah nodded, her mind already racing with possibilities. "It's risky, but we might not get another opportunity like this."

Matthew's jaw clenched. "We'll need to plan carefully. One wrong move and we could lose everything – or worse."

"Agreed," Sarah said, reaching for a fresh sheet of paper. "Let's map out every detail. We need to consider all angles, all potential outcomes."

As the night wore on, the three investigators huddled around the desk, their voices low and urgent. They sketched out plans, debated strategies, and accounted for every possible variable they could think of.

"Are we really ready for this?" Arthur asked, his voice tinged with doubt.

Sarah met his gaze, then Matthew's. She saw in their eyes the same mixture of fear and resolve that she felt in her own heart.

"We have to be," she said softly. "For Weymouth. For all the lives that have been lost. We can't let them continue."

Matthew nodded, reaching out to squeeze her hand. "Together, then?"

"Together," Sarah and Arthur echoed.

As the first light of dawn began to creep through the windows, a strange calm settled over Sarah. They had made their decision. Now, all that remained was to see it through.

RESOLVE

Matthew Fletcher stood at the edge of the harbour, his eyes fixed on the distant silhouette of South Point Lighthouse. The salty breeze ruffled his hair, carrying with it the aroma of the sea and the weight of his troubled thoughts. He'd spent countless hours investigating the shipwrecks and smuggling operations with Sarah, but lately, it felt like there was an ever-widening chasm between them, even as they were encroaching on what could crack the whole case open.

He watched as fishing boats bobbed gently in the water, their masts swaying in rhythm with the waves. The sight that once brought him comfort now only served to remind him of the turmoil in his heart. Sarah's increasing fascination with Ethan Blackwood gnawed at him, a constant ache that he could no longer ignore.

Matthew clenched his fists, remembering the way Sarah's eyes lit up when Ethan regaled her with tales of London society. The charming newcomer had swept into their lives like a whirlwind, offering Sarah glimpses of a world beyond Weymouth's shores. A world that Matthew feared he could never compete with.

He thought back to their shared moments – the late nights poring over documents, the thrill of uncovering each new piece of evidence, the moment at Nothe Fort when he was terrified he'd lost and then almost... But now, those moments seemed to be slipping away, replaced by Sarah's outings with Ethan to the Weymouth Pavilion and strolls along the Esplanade.

The realisation hit Matthew like a wave crashing against the rocks. He couldn't stand by and watch Sarah drift away, not without fighting for what they had. The thought of losing her to Ethan, to a life far from Weymouth, was unbearable.

With newfound determination, Matthew turned away from the harbour. His steps were quick and purposeful as he made his way towards the lighthouse. He had to tell Sarah how he felt, to lay bare the emotions he'd kept buried for so long. The time for hesitation was over.

MATTERS OF HEART AND DUTY

Sarah gripped the railing of the lighthouse balcony, her eyes on the horizon. Dark clouds roiled and churned, advancing like an army of shadows across the sky. The wind picked up, whistling through the ironwork and tugging at her skirts. She could taste the salt in the air, sharp and briny.

"Looks like we're in for a rough night," she muttered, tucking a wayward strand of hair behind her ear.

Sarah turned her attention to the lantern room. The Fresnel lens gleamed, its intricate array of prisms ready to magnify the light into a powerful beam. She checked the oil levels and trimmed the wick with practiced efficiency.

The first drops of rain began to patter against the glass as Sarah moved to secure the shutters. The wind howled around the lighthouse, a banshee's wail that set her nerves on edge. She wrestled with the heavy wooden panels, muscles straining as she latched them firmly in place.

Thunder rumbled in the distance, a low growl that seemed to shake the very foundations of the building. Sarah paused, her hand resting on the last shutter. For a moment, she was that frightened little girl again, alone and uncertain in a world that had taken everything from her.

She shook her head, banishing the memory. She wasn't that girl anymore. She was Sarah Campbell, assistant lighthouse keeper, protector of sailors, and an unraveler of mysteries.

The storm intensified, rain lashing against the windows in furious sheets. Sarah returned to the lantern, ensuring the flame burned bright and true. The beam cut through the darkness, a steady pulse of hope in the tempest.

Sarah's eyes darted down to the lighthouse door as it burst open, admitting a gust of wind and rain along with a soaked Matthew. His dark hair clung to his forehead, and water dripped from his sodden clothes, forming a puddle on the floor. Despite his bedraggled appearance, there was an intensity in his eyes that made Sarah's heart skip a beat.

Mr Thorne appeared behind Matthew, his weathered face creased with concern. "Matthew, lad, what brings you out in this tempest?"

Matthew's gaze locked onto Sarah, barely acknowledging Mr Thorne's presence. "I need to speak with Sarah," he said, his voice urgent. "It's important."

Sarah felt a flutter of anticipation. She and Matthew had been distant lately, their easy camaraderie strained by the presence of Ethan and their investigation. Yet here he was, braving the storm to see her.

Mr Thorne glanced between them, his keen eyes taking in the tension. With a slight nod, he stepped back. "Very well. I'll fetch some towels for you, Matthew. Can't have you catching your death."

As Mr Thorne retreated, Sarah moved closer to Matthew, drawn by the determination etched on his face. "Matthew, what is it? Has something happened with the investigation?"

Matthew shook his head, droplets of water flying from his

hair. "No, it's not that. It's—" He paused, seeming to struggle for words. "Sarah, I couldn't wait any longer. I had to tell you—"

A crack of thunder interrupted him. Sarah jumped, instinctively reaching out to steady herself. Her hand found Matthew's arm, and she felt the dampness of his sleeve, the warmth of his skin beneath.

The storm raged outside, lightning illuminating the room intermittently, casting dramatic shadows across Matthew's face. She could feel the heat radiating from his body, a stark contrast to the chill air that had followed him into the lighthouse.

The familiar scent of sea salt and weathered wood that clung to Matthew mingled with the sharp tang of rain. It stirred memories of their shared childhood, of long days spent exploring the shoreline and dreaming of adventures yet to come. Sarah found herself acutely aware of how much had changed since those carefree times, and yet how some things remained constant – like the steady presence of Matthew in her life.

Thunder rumbled overhead, its low growl seeming to reverberate through Sarah's chest. She watched as Matthew's hands clenched and unclenched, betraying his nervousness. The sight stirred a flutter of anticipation in her stomach. What could have driven him to brave such a tempest?

Matthew took a deep breath, his shoulders rising and falling with the effort. Sarah held her own breath. The air between them crackled with an energy that rivalled the storm outside.

"Sarah," Matthew began, his voice barely audible above the howling wind. He swallowed hard, Adam's apple bobbing in his throat. "I've been wanting to tell you..."

Another flash of lightning illuminated the room, throwing Matthew's features into sharp relief. Sarah saw the conflict in his eyes, the struggle between fear and resolve. She found herself reaching out, her hand hovering just shy of touching his arm, offering silent encouragement.

"Sarah, I can't keep this inside any longer," Matthew began again, his voice almost trembling over the sound of the storm. "I've loved you for a long time. More than just as a friend."

The words hit Sarah like a physical force, stealing her breath away. She watched, mesmerised, as Matthew's face transformed. The hesitation and nervousness melted away, replaced by a fierce determination.

"Do you remember that day at the fair, when we first met?" Matthew asked, his words tumbling out in a rush. "Even then, I felt something special. Your strength, your kindness – it amazed me. And as we grew up together, solving this mystery, my admiration only grew."

Sarah's mind whirled, memories flashing before her. She saw Matthew as a boy at the fair, his infectious laugh as they shared candied apples. She remembered countless hours spent huddled over documents, their heads bent close as they unravelled clues. The night at Nothe Fort replayed in vivid detail – the fear, the exhilaration, and the moment Matthew had pulled her to safety. Each moment took on new meaning, illuminated by Matthew's confession.

"Your intelligence, your courage – they inspire me every day," Matthew continued, his voice growing stronger. "The way you've overcome so much, how you've made a place for yourself here. Sarah, you're the bravest person I know."

Tears pricked at Sarah's eyes, threatening to spill over. She had never heard Matthew speak like this before, with such raw honesty and passion. It stirred something deep within her, a feeling she had pushed aside for so long, afraid to examine it too closely.

"When I'm with you, I feel like I can face anything," Matthew said, taking a step closer. "We've been through so much together, and there's no one else I'd rather have by my side. You understand me in a way no one else does."

Sarah's world narrowed to a pinpoint, her senses overwhelmed by Matthew's proximity and the weight of his words. The storm outside faded to a distant rumble, drowned out by the thundering of her own heart. Matthew's hands were warm and calloused against hers, a familiar touch that now sent sparks racing up her arms.

She stared into Matthew's eyes, seeing the vulnerability and hope shimmering there. The raw honesty in his voice had stripped away all pretence, leaving her faced with a truth she'd been avoiding for so long.

Matthew's hands enveloped hers. His touch, so familiar yet suddenly electric, sent a shiver through her body.

"You mean everything to me, Sarah," Matthew said, his voice softening. The words seemed to hang in the air between them, weighted with years of unspoken feelings. "I'd do anything to see you happy."

Sarah felt her heart racing a thunderous beat.

Matthew's grip on her hands tightened slightly, his eyes searching her face. "Please," he said, his voice thick with emotion, "tell me there's a chance… that you feel the same."

Matthew's hands slipped away as Sarah gently withdrew her own. The loss of contact left her feeling suddenly cold, exposed to the chill air that seeped through the lighthouse walls. She looked into Matthew's eyes, seeing the hope there begin to falter, and her heart clenched painfully in her chest.

"Matthew, I…" Sarah's voice caught. She swallowed hard, trying to find the right words. "I care for you deeply, but I'm not sure if it's the same way you feel about me."

The words hung heavy in the air between them. Sarah watched as Matthew's expression shifted, hope giving way to confusion and hurt. She wanted to reach out, to offer some comfort, but she held herself back, knowing it would only make things more difficult.

"This investigation, the smuggling ring…" Sarah continued,

her voice wavering. "Everything is so overwhelming. I don't think I can think clearly about anything else right now."

Sarah wrapped her arms around herself, feeling small and vulnerable.

"There's so much at stake," Sarah said softly. "So many lives depending on us uncovering the truth. I can't let myself be distracted, not when we're so close to exposing the conspiracy."

She looked away from Matthew, her gaze drawn to the Fresnel lens. The steady beam of light cutting through the darkness outside seemed to mock her inner confusion. Sarah had always prided herself on her clarity of purpose, her ability to guide others to safety. But now, faced with Matthew's declaration, she felt utterly lost.

Matthew took a step back, his shoulders slumping as if under an invisible weight.

"I... I'm sorry," Matthew mumbled. He turned abruptly, fumbling with the door handle. Sarah stood frozen, unable to find the words to stop him as he stepped back out into the driving rain.

The sound of the door closing behind Matthew echoed through the lighthouse, a finality that made Sarah flinch. She rushed to the window, pressing her hands against the cold glass as she watched Matthew's figure disappear into the storm. The rain lashed against the panes, blurring her vision, but she couldn't tear her eyes away.

As Matthew vanished from sight, the full weight of what had just transpired settled upon Sarah. She slid down to the floor, her back against the door, and wrapped her arms around her knees. The lighthouse suddenly felt cavernous and empty, the absence of Matthew's presence leaving a void she hadn't expected.

Sarah's mind whirled with conflicting emotions. She cared for Matthew deeply, that much she knew. But was it love? The kind of love he spoke of with such passion and certainty? She thought of Ethan, of the excitement and new experiences he represented. Then she thought of Matthew, steady and true, who had been by her side through so much.

Sarah remained on the floor, her back pressed against the cold wood of the door. The storm raged outside, but it was nothing compared to the tempest in her heart. She barely registered the sound of footsteps approaching.

"Sarah, my dear," Mr Thorne's gruff voice was tinged with concern.

"It's Matthew," Sarah whispered. "He... he told me he loves me."

Mr Thorne nodded slowly. "And how do you feel about that?"

Sarah hugged her knees tighter to her chest. "I don't know," she admitted. "I care for Matthew, I truly do. But with everything that's happening... I just can't think clearly about it all."

She glanced at Mr Thorne, seeking some sign of understanding in his weathered face. "I told him I wasn't sure if I felt the same way. That I couldn't be distracted right now. And he left, out into the storm."

Mr Thorne's eyes softened with sympathy. He reached out, placing a hand on Sarah's shoulder. "Matters of the heart are never simple, lass. Especially not when mixed up with matters of duty."

Sarah leaned into the comforting touch, grateful for Mr Thorne's steady presence. "I feel like I've hurt him," she confessed. "But I couldn't lie to him either. What if I've ruined everything between us?"

Mr Thorne settled himself beside Sarah, his joints creaking as he lowered himself to the floor.

"Lass," Mr Thorne began, "true friendship isn't so easily broken. What you and Matthew have weathered storms far worse than this."

Sarah lifted her head, meeting Mr Thorne's kind gaze. His

eyes, the colour of storm-tossed seas, held a wisdom that came from years of guiding ships through treacherous waters.

"But what if I've pushed him away for good?"

Mr Thorne chuckled softly, the sound rumbling deep in his chest. "Matthew Fletcher isn't the type to abandon ship at the first sign of rough seas. He's made of sterner stuff than that."

He reached out, patting Sarah's hand with his own weathered one. "You've both been through so much together. This investigation, the dangers you've faced – it's bound to stir up all sorts of feelings. There's no shame in needing time to sort them out."

A small spark of hope ignited within Sarah. Mr Thorne's words, as always, seemed to cut through the fog of her confusion, offering a clear path forward.

"The heart's a tricky thing," Mr Thorne continued, his gaze drifting to the window where rain lashed against the glass. "It doesn't always beat in time with our plans or our duties. But that doesn't mean we should ignore it entirely."

He turned back to Sarah, a small smile crinkling the corners of his eyes. "Give yourself time, lass. And give Matthew time too. The truth of your feelings will come clear, just like the dawn after a long night's watch."

∼

MATTHEW STUMBLED through the door of his small fishing cabin, water dripping from his clothes and forming puddles on the worn wooden floor. He barely noticed the chill that had seeped into his bones, his mind consumed by the ache in his heart.

The cabin felt emptier than ever as he stood there, staring out the rain-streaked window at the raging storm. Lightning flashed across the sky, illuminating the churning waves of Weymouth Bay. It was a fitting backdrop for the turmoil within.

Sarah's face swam before his eyes, her expression of uncertainty etched into his memory. He'd laid his heart bare, hoping against hope that she'd reciprocate his feelings. But her hesitation had cut deeper than any knife could.

Matthew's hands clenched into fists at his sides. He'd been a fool to think she'd choose him over the worldly Ethan Blackwood. What did he have to offer her? A life of hard work and salt-stained hands? How could that compare to the glittering world Ethan promised?

He slumped into a chair, burying his face in his hands. The investigation that had brought them so close now felt like a chasm between them. He'd thought their shared purpose, their determination to uncover the truth, had forged an unbreakable bond. But perhaps he'd been reading too much into their friendship all along.

A sob caught in Matthew's throat. He'd known Sarah since they were children, had watched her grow from a grief-stricken orphan into a strong, capable woman. He'd fallen in love with her spirit, her kindness, her unwavering dedication to helping others. And now, that love was a source of nothing but pain and confusion.

PART III
LOVE'S TRUE HARBOUR

1866-1867

SHADOWS OVER THE REGATTA

~~~~

The streets of Weymouth buzzed with excitement as Sarah made her way through the town. Colourful banners fluttered overhead, their vibrant hues set against the grey clouds that threatened rain. Stalls sprang up like mushrooms along the Esplanade, their owners busily arranging wares and setting out signs. The air was thick with sea-salt and anticipation.

Sarah paused at the harbour's edge, watching as boats were meticulously prepared for the grand summer regatta. Sails unfurled in the breeze, snapping taut as if eager to catch the wind. Deckhands scurried about, their voices carrying across the water in a cacophony of shouts and laughter.

Yet despite the palpable excitement that gripped the town, Sarah found little joy in the festivities. Her mind was consumed by their investigation and the looming confrontation with the smuggling ring. She glanced at Matthew, who stood a few paces away, his gaze fixed on the horizon.

The distance between them felt insurmountable. Matthew's confession of love hung in the air like a fog, obscuring the easy camaraderie they once shared. Sarah longed to bridge the gap, to find the words that would mend their fractured friendship, but every attempt died on her lips.

Matthew turned, catching her eye for a brief moment before looking away. His jaw was set, shoulders tense beneath his worn jacket. He seemed a stranger to her now, so far removed from the boy who'd shared her grief and dreams all those years ago.

With a deep breath, Sarah turned away, her light blue eyes scanning the crowd. She caught sight of Ethan Blackwood's tall figure near the Pavilion, his easy charm drawing a small gathering of admirers. A flutter of excitement stirred within her, quickly followed by a stab of guilt.

"This won't do," Sarah muttered to herself, shaking her head as if to clear away the conflicting emotions. She reached into her pocket, fingers brushing against the rough edges of one of the coded messages they'd deciphered. The smuggling ring – that was where her focus needed to be.

As she made her way through the throng of people, Sarah's mind raced with possibilities. The upcoming regatta would provide the perfect cover for the smugglers' activities, but it also presented an opportunity to catch them red-handed. She found herself analysing every face she passed, wondering who might be involved in the nefarious plot.

Later that evening, Sarah pored over the documents spread across the table. Mr Thorne's presence nearby offered some comfort, but it couldn't dispel the worry that clouded her eyes. She traced the connections they'd uncovered, her finger moving from name to name: Wentworth, Leighton, Collins.

"We're so close," she murmured, more to herself than to Mr Thorne. "But who's behind it all?"

As she worked, Sarah couldn't help but think of Matthew and Ethan. The guilt of her unresolved feelings gnawed at her, threatening to distract her from the task at hand. She longed for the simplicity of her childhood, when the lighthouse had been her whole world and her path had seemed so clear.

⁓

MATTHEW HUNCHED over the rickety table in his fishing cabin, his fingers tracing the lines of a weathered map. The soft glow of a lantern cast long shadows across the room, illuminating the determination etched on his face.

Scattered around him lay a sea of papers – coded messages, shipping manifests, and hastily scribbled notes. Each one a piece of the puzzle he was desperately trying to solve. The investigation had become his anchor, keeping him tethered to reality as his heart threatened to drift away on a tide of unrequited love.

"There's got to be a connection," he muttered, running a hand through his tousled hair. The gesture, once playful, now seemed born of frustration. He reached for another document, his movements fuelled by a mix of protective instinct and the need to fill the void left by Sarah's uncertain response to his confession.

The creaking of the cabin's timbers in the night wind seemed to echo the ache in his chest. But Matthew pushed the pain aside, focusing instead on the intricate web of deceit they'd uncovered. His fingers ghosted over the list of names he and Sarah had compiled – Wentworth, Leighton, Collins – each one a thread in the tapestry of corruption threatening to unravel Weymouth.

A sudden gust rattled the window, drawing Matthew's attention to the world outside. The moon peeked through the clouds, casting a silvery glow on the harbour. For a moment, he allowed himself to imagine Sarah standing at the lighthouse, her auburn hair catching the moonlight. The image sent a pang through his heart, but it also steeled his resolve.

"I'll protect you, Sarah," he whispered to the empty room. "Even if you don't love me back."

With renewed determination, Matthew turned back to his work. He poured over shipping schedules, cross-referencing them with the coded messages they'd intercepted. His mind, usually filled with thoughts of the sea and its bounty, now navigated the treacherous waters of conspiracy and deceit.

A WHISPER IN THE CROWD

Sarah stood at the lighthouse window, her gaze on the harbour where Matthew's fishing boat bobbed gently in the water. A sigh escaped her lips as she contemplated their decision to pursue separate leads in their investigation.

Donning her best dress, Sarah made her way to the Weymouth Pavilion. The grand building loomed before her, its opulent facade a stark contrast to the simple life she'd known. She took a deep breath, smoothing her skirts before ascending the steps.

Inside, the Pavilion buzzed with activity. Ladies in fine silks twirled across the dance floor, and gentlemen engaged in hushed conversations over glasses of champagne. Sarah's eyes darted from face to face, searching for any sign of suspicious behaviour.

She caught sight of Beatrice Wentworth and Jonathan Leighton huddled in a corner, their heads bent close in fervent discussion. Sarah's pulse quickened as she edged closer, straining to catch snippets of their conversation.

"The shipment must not be delayed. The boss won't like it one bit." Wentworth muttered.

Leighton nodded, his eyes darting nervously around the room. "Leave him to me, I'll soothe is nerves, making him less prickly. And what of our friend in London? Has he secured the necessary documents?"

Sarah's mind raced, piecing together the fragments of information. She was so engrossed in her eavesdropping that she nearly jumped when a hand touched her elbow.

"Sarah!" Ethan's smooth voice sent a shiver down her spine. "I didn't expect to see you here this evening."

Sarah turned, forcing a smile onto her face. "Ethan, what a pleasant surprise."

As Ethan led her away from Wentworth and Leighton, Sarah couldn't help but wonder if his timely interruption was mere coincidence or something more sinister. She allowed him to guide her through the crowd, all the while keeping her senses alert for any further clues that might unravel the mystery surrounding Weymouth's smuggling ring.

REFLECTIONS AT SEA

Leaning against the weathered wooden railing of the harbour, Matthew's eyes scanned the darkened waters. The night air carried the salty scent of the sea, mingling with the pungent aroma of tobacco and ale wafting from the nearby taverns. He'd been spending more evenings here lately, ears pricked for any whisper of information about the recent shipwrecks.

"Aye, it's not natural," old Tom muttered, joining Matthew at the railing. "Never seen so many wrecks in such calm waters."

Matthew nodded. "Something's amiss, that's for certain."

As the night wore on, Matthew made his rounds, stopping to chat with the grizzled fishermen mending their nets and the rowdy sailors spilling out of The Rusty Anchor. Fragments of conversation reached his ears, each one adding to the growing unease in his gut.

"Heard there's a big shipment coming in," a red-faced sailor slurred, swaying on his feet. "During the regatta, they say. When all eyes'll be on them fancy boats."

Matthew's ears perked up. "A shipment, you say? What sort?"

The sailor shrugged, nearly losing his balance. "Dunno. But it's worth a pretty penny, that's for sure."

As Matthew made his way back to his small fishing boat, his mind raced. A high-stakes shipment during the regatta – it fit the pattern they'd uncovered. But who was behind it all?

With each passing day, the danger seemed to grow. Matthew's resolve hardened. He'd protect his town, protect Sarah, no matter the cost. As he cast off his mooring lines and set out for a night of fishing, Matthew's eyes scanned the horizon, watchful for any sign of the treachery lurking in Weymouth's waters.

∽

THE VAST EXPANSE of the sea stretched out before Matthew, a canvas of deep blues and greys.

As he cast his nets into the churning waters, Matthew's thoughts couldn't help but turn once again to the investigation. Every new piece of information they uncovered felt like a double-edged sword. On one hand, they were getting closer to the truth, to protecting Weymouth and its people. On the other, each step forward seemed to put Sarah in greater danger. The thought of harm coming to her made his stomach churn more violently than any rough sea ever could.

The sun dipped low on the horizon, painting the sky in hues of orange and pink. Matthew barely noticed the beauty, his mind consumed with worry and longing. He mechanically went through the motions of hauling in his catch, his movements lacking their usual vigour.

As he steered the boat back to harbour, Matthew caught sight of his reflection in a rain barrel. The man staring back at him looked older, more careworn. Unspoken words and unrequited love had etched lines around his eyes that hadn't been there before.

"You're back late," a familiar voice called out as Matthew tied up his boat. His father, Harold Fletcher, stood on the dock, concern evident in his features.

Matthew nodded, managing a small smile that didn't reach his eyes. "Aye, the fish were being stubborn today."

Harold studied his son for a long moment. "It's not just the fish troubling you, is it, lad?"

Matthew hesitated, then shook his head. He couldn't bring himself to burden his father with the full weight of his troubles, but neither could he deny the truth of his words.

Harold placed a comforting hand on Matthew's shoulder. "It will all be all right in the end, and if things aren't all right, right now, it means it isn't the end. The Lord always has a plan for us, and if we follow where he leads, then all shall be well."

Matthew wanted to believe his father, to find comfort in his dad's wisdom, but his worries pressed down on him like an anchor.

"Thanks, Pa," he managed, his voice gruff with emotion. "I'll keep that in mind."

Harold squeezed his son's shoulder once more before releasing him. "Come on then, let's get this catch sorted. No use letting good fish go to waste while we stand here chin-wagging."

Together, they set about unloading Matthew's boat. The familiar routine of sorting and cleaning the fish provided a welcome distraction from the tumult in Matthew's mind. As they worked, Harold regaled him with tales of his own youthful misadventures, each story punctuated by his hearty chuckle.

Despite himself, Matthew found a smile tugging at the corners of his mouth.

As they finished up, Matthew caught sight of a figure hurrying along the harbour front. Even in the fading light, he'd recognise that silhouette anywhere. Sarah.

His heart leapt, then immediately sank as he saw who she

was with. Ethan Blackwood, looking every inch the dashing gentleman in his fine coat and hat.

Matthew's hands clenched involuntarily, his knuckles white around the handle of his fish basket. He watched as Sarah laughed at something Ethan said, her head tilted back in mirth.

"You all right there, lad?" Harold's voice cut through the fog of Matthew's thoughts.

Matthew blinked, realising he'd been staring. "Yeah, Pa. Just... just tired is all."

Harold followed his son's gaze, but he said nothing.

TROUBLE IN THE TEA ROOM

Sarah walked into the Wentworth Tea Room, her eyes scanning the elegant surroundings. The soft clink of china and hushed conversations filled the air as she made her way to a corner table. She had come here under the guise of enjoying afternoon tea, but her true purpose was far more clandestine.

As she sipped her tea, Sarah observed Beatrice Wentworth bustling about the room, her perfectly coiffed hair and impeccable manners in opposition with the suspicions Sarah harboured. When Beatrice disappeared into the back room, Sarah saw her opportunity.

Feigning a need for the powder room, Sarah slipped behind the counter and into the small office at the rear of the tea room. Her heart pounded as she quickly rifled through drawers and cabinets, searching for anything out of the ordinary.

Just as she was about to give up, Sarah's fingers brushed against something hidden beneath a stack of receipts. She pulled out a leather-bound ledger, its pages filled with neat columns of numbers and cryptic notations.

Sarah's breath caught as she flipped through the pages. The

ledger was a meticulous record of transactions, each entry carefully coded but unmistakably detailing shipments and payments that far exceeded the scope of a simple tea room.

"Well, well," Beatrice's voice cut through the silence, causing Sarah to jump. "It seems our little lighthouse keeper has developed quite the curiosity."

Sarah whirled around, the ledger clutched to her chest, her mind racing for an explanation. But Beatrice's knowing smirk told her that no excuse would suffice.

"Mrs Wentworth," Sarah began, her voice steadier than she felt. "I do apologise for the intrusion. I was looking for a pen to jot down a recipe I overheard at one of the tables. Your scones are simply divine, and I hoped to recreate them for Mr Thorne."

Beatrice's eyes narrowed, clearly unconvinced. "And that required rifling through my private papers?"

Sarah forced a sheepish laugh. "Oh, goodness no! I'm afraid in my eagerness, I became quite clumsy. I knocked over a stack of papers and was just trying to set them right when you came in." She gestured vaguely at the desk. "I'm terribly embarrassed by my clumsiness."

Beatrice took a step closer, her gaze fixed on the ledger Sarah held. "And what, pray tell, is that you're clutching so tightly?"

Sarah's mind whirled. She loosened her grip on the ledger, affecting nonchalance. "This? Why, it's my own notebook. I always carry it with me for jotting down lighthouse observations and such. Force of habit, I'm afraid."

She slipped the ledger into her bag, praying Beatrice wouldn't demand to see it. "I really am sorry for the disturbance, Mrs Wentworth. Perhaps I could make it up to you by helping in the kitchen sometime? I do miss my days in the bakery."

Beatrice's expression softened slightly, though suspicion still lingered in her eyes. "That won't be necessary, Miss Campbell. But do remember that private areas are just that – private."

Sarah nodded, edging towards the door. "Of course, Mrs Wentworth. It won't happen again. Thank you for your understanding."

With a final apologetic smile, Sarah slipped past Beatrice and out of the office. She forced herself to walk calmly through the tea room, nodding politely to other patrons, all the while feeling Beatrice's gaze boring into her back.

A GLIMPSE OF CORRUPTION

Matthew trudged through the narrow streets of Weymouth, his mind a whirlwind.

As he rounded a corner, the sound of hushed voices caught his attention. Matthew pressed himself against the rough brick wall of a nearby building, his heart pounding in his chest. He peered around the edge, his eyes widening at the sight before him.

There, in a secluded alley barely lit by the dim glow of a single gas lamp, stood Reverend Edward Collins. The parish priest's usually serene face was twisted with an expression Matthew had never seen before - a mixture of anxiety and determination.

"The payments must be made on time," Collins hissed to two shadowy figures whose faces Matthew couldn't make out. "We can't afford any mistakes, not with the regatta approaching. *He* won't have it!"

Matthew's breath caught in his throat. He used to respect the Reverend; he knew his father had found much solace in the Reverend's sermons after the passing of his wife, with Matthew just a babe in his arms. To see the Reverend now, clearly involved in something nefarious, sent a chill down Matthew's spine.

One of the figures spoke. "And the logistics? Everything's in place?"

Collins nodded, glancing furtively over his shoulder. Matthew ducked back, pressing himself flat against the wall, his heart hammering so loudly he feared it might give him away.

"Yes, yes," the Reverend replied impatiently. "The shipment will arrive as planned. Just make sure your men are ready."

THE GATHERING STORM

Weymouth's grand summer regatta was mere days away, and the town buzzed with anticipation. But for Sarah, the excitement was tinged with a sense of impending danger.

She turned to face Matthew and Arthur Finch, who were hunched over a table strewn with documents, maps, and hastily scribbled notes.

"We've got to be certain," Sarah said, her voice tight with determination. "Once we make our move, there's no going back."

Matthew looked up, his eyes reflecting a mix of resolve and barely concealed hurt. "We've triple-checked everything. The shipment will arrive during the regatta, hidden among the influx of visitors and competing vessels."

Arthur nodded, his fingers tracing a line on one of the maps. "The postal records confirm it. They've been using my system to coordinate their activities right under our noses."

Sarah approached the table, her mind racing. "So we split up. Matthew, you'll monitor the harbour. I'll keep an eye on Beatrice Wentworth and Jonathan Leighton at the Pavilion. And Arthur—"

"I'll intercept any last-minute messages they might try to send," Arthur finished, a glimmer of excitement in his eyes.

As they finalised their plans, Sarah couldn't help but think of Ethan. His charm and worldliness had opened her eyes to possibilities beyond Weymouth, but now doubt gnawed at her. His timely appearances during crucial moments of their investigation seemed too convenient to be coincidental.

"What about Ethan?" Matthew asked, voicing Sarah's unspoken concern. "He's been awfully interested in our coming and going."

Sarah hesitated, torn between her growing suspicions and the warmth she felt in Ethan's presence. "I'll... I'll keep him close during the regatta. If he's involved, we can't risk him catching wind of our plans."

Matthew's jaw tightened, but he nodded curtly. Sarah saw the pain in his eyes, a reflection of the confession she'd been unable to reciprocate. She wanted to reach out, but their mission held her back.

As the group dispersed, each to make their final preparations, Sarah was alone in the lantern room. She gazed out at the sea, the lighthouse beam sweeping across the darkening waters. The regatta would be their moment of truth, a chance to protect Weymouth and bring justice to those who had caused so much suffering.

With a shaky breath, Sarah steeled herself for the challenges ahead. Whatever the outcome, she knew that Weymouth's fate – and perhaps her own – would be forever changed by the events of the coming days.

HIGH STAKES AT THE HARBOUR

The air thrummed with excitement, a cacophony of laughter, cheers, and the flapping of colourful flags in the breeze. The Weymouth Summer Regatta was in full swing. Boats of every size and description bobbed in the harbour, their masts creating a forest of wood and canvas against the cloudless sky.

Sarah's heart raced, not from the festive atmosphere, but from the task that lay before her. She glanced at Matthew, who was mingling with the crowds just a little ways along, his eyes whipping across the harbour.

As she wove through the throng of merrymakers, Sarah's eyes darted from face to face, searching for any sign of her targets. Beatrice Wentworth's elegant silhouette, or Jonathan Leighton's distinctive gait.

Matthew's hand brushed against hers as they passed one another, a fleeting touch that spoke volumes. Despite the strain in their relationship, their shared purpose bound them together. They moved in sync, two hunters amidst a sea of revellers, biding their time.

Sarah's fingers ghosted over the hidden pocket in her skirts, feeling the outline of one of the secrets notes they had discovered. Just one piece of the plethora of evidence they had amassed. The evidence that could bring down the smuggling ring and save countless lives. She steeled herself for the moment when they would need to act.

As she neared the harbour's edge, Sarah caught sight of Arthur Finch in the distance, his eyes meeting hers in a silent acknowledgment. Their plan was in motion, the pieces falling into place amidst the chaos of the regatta.

Sarah caught sight of Beatrice Wentworth's elegant silhouette near the edge of the pier. The tea room owner's usually composed demeanour seemed ruffled, her gestures more animated than usual. Beside her stood Jonathan Leighton, his face set in a grim mask of concern.

Sarah edged closer, feigning interest in a nearby display of maritime knots. She tilted her head, straining to catch their words over the din of the crowd.

"This is madness, Jonathan," Beatrice hissed, her voice barely above a whisper. "Hargrave's pushing too far. If this goes wrong—"

"Keep your voice down," Leighton growled, his eyes darting nervously. "Reginald knows what he's doing. He's kept us safe this long."

Reginald Hargrave - the respected magistrate? Her mind raced, pieces of the puzzle suddenly snapping into place.

Beatrice's voice rose, tinged with panic. "But the shipment tonight - it's too risky. Hargrave's gambling with all our necks!"

"Enough!" Leighton grabbed Beatrice's arm, his knuckles white. "Remember who put this whole operation together. Reginald Hargrave isn't a man to be crossed."

Sarah's heart pounded, blood rushing in her ears. Reginald Hargrave - the mastermind behind it all. The final piece they'd been searching for. She needed to find Matthew, now.

She turned, ready to seek out Matthew and share this crucial piece of information, when a familiar figure stepped into her path.

Ethan stood before her, but gone was his usual charming smile. His eyes were cold, his jaw set in a hard line that sent a chill down Sarah's spine.

"Sarah, my dear," Ethan's voice was low, menacing. "I'm afraid we need to have a little chat."

Before Sarah could react, Ethan's hand shot out, gripping her arm with bruising force. She gasped, more from shock than pain, as he began to drag her through the crowd.

"Ethan, what are you doing?" Sarah hissed, trying to wrench her arm free. But his grip was like iron, unyielding as he pulled her towards the docks.

People jostled around them, too caught up in the regatta's excitement to notice Sarah's distress. She opened her mouth to cry out, but Ethan leaned in close, his breath hot against her ear.

"I wouldn't do that if I were you," he growled. "Unless you want your dear Matthew to suffer the consequences."

Sarah's blood ran cold. She stumbled along beside Ethan, her mind reeling as they approached one of the racing yachts. With a forceful shove, Ethan propelled her onto the deck.

Her head spun as Ethan rapidly undid the knots of the heavy ropes holding the yacht in the harbour.

As the yacht began to pull away from the harbour, Sarah's panic surged. She gripped the railing, her knuckles white, watching the distance grow between her and the safety of the shore. The regatta crowds grew smaller, their cheers fading as the wind carried them out to sea.

Sarah turned to face Ethan, her light blue eyes blazing with a mixture of fear and defiance. "What is the meaning of this?" she demanded, her voice shaking despite her best efforts to remain calm.

Ethan's lips curled into a cruel smile. "Oh, Sarah," he said, advancing towards her. "You've been quite the nuisance, you know. Poking your nose where it doesn't belong. I'm afraid I can't allow that to continue."

Ethan drawled, his voice dripping with disdain. "You've made this all too easy. Did you really think a simple lighthouse girl could catch the eye of a London gentleman?" Ethan forcefully slipped a rope around Sarah's wrists and tugged. It pulled into a tight knot, slamming her hands together. "A little sailing trick I picked up." Ethan taunted. "Do you think your little Matthew would be impressed?"

He circled her like a predator, his movements fluid and menacing. Sarah struggled against the rope that bound her wrists, the rough hemp biting into her skin.

"You were so eager for a taste of sophistication, weren't you?" Ethan taunted, his fingers trailing along her cheek in a mockery of affection. "So desperate to believe that someone like me could genuinely care for you."

Sarah flinched away from his touch, her cheeks burning with shame and anger. How could she have been so blind?

Ethan's laugh, once smooth and charming, now grated on her ears like broken glass. "I must admit, it was almost too easy. A few pretty words, some tales of London society, and you were putty in my hands."

He leaned in close, his breath hot against her ear. "Did you enjoy our little outings, Sarah? The theatre, the parties? All carefully orchestrated to keep you distracted while we went about our real business."

"I know all about it!" Sarah almost spat at him. "I know Reginald Hargrave is behind the whole thing!"

"You are very clever. But I'm afraid just not quite clever enough." Ethan said, his voice taking on a lecturing tone, "I'm not just some random gentleman from London. I'm Reginald Hargrave's nephew, his eyes and ears in the capital. The perfect liaison between our London contacts and our Weymouth operation."

He clicked his tongue, shaking his head in mock disappointment. "And you, my curious little lighthouse keeper, have been causing quite a stir. Stealing Mrs Wentworth's ledger? Tsk tsk, Sarah. So clumsy. Did you really think we wouldn't notice?"

Sarah struggled against her bonds, the rough hemp digging into her wrists as the yacht pitched and rolled beneath her feet.

"You won't get away with this," Sarah said, her voice trembling with a mixture of fear and defiance. "People will notice I'm missing. Matthew—"

Ethan's laugh cut through her words like a knife. "Oh, Sarah. Your faith in that simple fisherman is touching, really. But he's no match for what we have in store."

The yacht lurched suddenly, nearly sending Sarah stumbling. She caught herself against the railing, her eyes darting to the churning waves below. The regatta and Weymouth's familiar shoreline had faded to a distant smudge on the horizon.

"What do you want from me?" Sarah demanded, forcing steel into her voice despite the terror clawing at her insides.

Ethan's eyes glinted with cruel amusement. "Want? My dear, you've already given us everything we need. Your meddling has forced our hand, accelerated our plans. Tonight's shipment will be our biggest yet, and you won't be around to interfere."

He stepped closer, his fingers tracing the line of her jaw in a mockery of tenderness. "It's almost a shame, really. You could have been quite useful if you weren't so stubbornly moral."

Sarah jerked away from his touch, disgust roiling in her stomach. "I'd rather die than help you destroy lives for profit," she spat.

"That," Ethan said, his voice dropping to a menacing whisper, "can certainly be arranged."

RACE THROUGH THE STORM

∞

Matthew's eyes darted across the bustling regatta, searching for any sign of Sarah. The festive atmosphere did nothing to quell the unease gnawing at his gut. Something was amiss, he could feel it in his bones.

He pushed through the throng of revellers, his muscular frame tense with worry. The salty air that usually invigorated him now seemed oppressive, clouding his senses. Where was she?

"Blimey, watch where you're going!" An elderly gentleman exclaimed as Matthew accidentally bumped into him.

"Sorry, sir," Matthew muttered, barely breaking stride.

He scanned the faces in the crowd, hoping to catch a glimpse of Sarah. But she was nowhere to be found.

His gaze swept across the harbour, taking in the colourful flags and banners adorning the ships. That's when he saw it – a yacht pulling away from the dock, its sails unfurling in the breeze.

Matthew's heart plummeted. There, at the helm, stood Ethan Blackwood, his refined posture unmistakable even from a distance. And on the deck, a figure with flowing auburn hair struggled against unseen bonds.

Sarah.

A surge of protective fury coursed through Matthew's veins. He clenched his fists, his knuckles turning white with the force of his grip. Without a second thought, he sprinted towards the water's edge, his mind racing to formulate a plan.

The yacht was gaining speed, cutting through the waves. Matthew knew he had to act fast. He glanced around frantically, searching for anything that could help him reach Sarah.

The sky started to darken ominously. The once-cheerful atmosphere of the regatta quickly turned to chaos as dark clouds rolled in, blotting out the sun. Revellers cried out in dismay, their festive mood shattered by the sudden change in weather.

"The storm's coming in fast," he muttered, his eyes never leaving the yacht that carried Sarah away.

Without hesitation, Matthew sprinted to his small fishing boat. He untied it with practiced ease, his hands working swiftly despite the trembling urgency. As he pushed off from the dock, the first drops of rain began to fall, pattering against the wooden hull.

The sea, which had been calm just moments ago, now churned with growing fury. Matthew gripped the tiller, his knuckles white with determination. He had navigated these waters countless times, but never under such dire circumstances.

As he steered his vessel through the turbulent bay, Matthew's eyes remained fixed on the racing yacht ahead. The wind whipped at his face, and salt spray stung his eyes, but he barely noticed. His entire being was focused on reaching Sarah.

"Hold on," he whispered, willing his words to reach her somehow. "I'm coming for you."

The storm intensified, waves crashing against the side of his small craft. But Matthew held steady, his years of experience evident in every adjustment he made. He leaned into the wind, using its force to propel him forward rather than hinder his progress.

As he drew nearer to the yacht, Matthew could make out Sarah's figure on the deck. Even from a distance, he could see her struggling against her bonds. The sight filled him with a mixture of relief and renewed determination.

"Just a little closer," he urged his boat, as if it could understand his desperation.

Matthew manoeuvred his small fishing boat alongside the yacht. The storm raged around them, wind howling and waves crashing against both vessels. He gripped the side of his boat, muscles tensed, waiting for the perfect moment.

The deck of the yacht rose and fell with the turbulent sea, but Matthew's keen eyes tracked its movement. He'd made countless leaps from boat to boat in his life, but never with such high stakes.

Sarah's muffled cries reached his ears over the tempest, spurring him on. He saw her on the deck, hands bound, desperately trying to signal for help.

"Now," Matthew muttered to himself.

As the yacht dipped low, Matthew launched himself from his fishing boat. For a heart-stopping moment, he was airborne, the angry sea churning beneath him. Then his feet hit the deck with a solid thud, his knees bending to absorb the impact.

He straightened up, salt water streaming from his soaked clothes. The familiar roll of a ship's deck beneath his feet steadied him, even as the storm raged on.

Ethan stood at the helm, his usually impeccable appearance now dishevelled by the wind and rain. He'd been focused on Sarah, trying to stop her frantic signalling. At the sound of

Matthew's landing, Ethan whirled around, his green eyes widening in shock.

For a moment, the two men locked gazes, the air between them charged with tension despite the chaos of the storm.

THE STORM'S FURY

Sarah watched in horror as Matthew and Ethan collided on the deck of the yacht. The two men grappled fiercely, their bodies silhouetted against the darkening sky. Lightning flashed, illuminating the scene in stark relief.

Matthew's face was a mask of determination, his jaw set and eyes blazing with protective fury. He lunged at Ethan, tackling him to the deck with a resounding thud. Ethan, caught off guard by Matthew's sudden appearance, fought back with desperate intensity.

The yacht pitched and rolled beneath them as the storm raged. Waves crashed over the sides, drenching the combatants. Sarah struggled against her bonds as she watched the men locked in mortal combat.

Ethan, his refined facade shattered, lashed out with surprising strength. His fist connected with Matthew's jaw, sending the fisherman reeling. But Matthew, hardened by years of labour at sea, absorbed the blow and came back swinging.

The two men traded punches, their grunts of exertion clashing with the howling wind. Sarah could see the raw emotion etched on Matthew's face – love, fear, and fierce protectiveness all warring for dominance.

Ethan, realising he was outmatched in brute strength, scrabbled for a weapon. His hand closed around a loose piece of rigging, and he swung it wildly at Matthew's head. Matthew ducked, the makeshift club whistling past his ear.

In that moment, Sarah saw the depths of Ethan's desperation. The charming gentleman she thought she knew was gone, replaced by a cornered animal fighting for survival. The realisation sent a chill through her, colder than the rain lashing her skin.

Matthew pressed his advantage, driving Ethan back across the deck with a flurry of blows. The yacht lurched violently, nearly sending both men overboard. They grappled at the railing, each trying to gain the upper hand as the storm raged around them.

Sarah's eyes fell upon a lantern secured to the mast, its flame flickering wildly in the storm. A spark of hope ignited within her. Years of working alongside Mr Thorne had taught her more than just the mechanics of keeping the light burning – she knew how to communicate with it.

Sarah twisted her body, inching closer to the lantern despite her bound hands. The ropes bit into her wrists, but she ignored the pain, focused solely on her goal. She manoeuvred herself into position, using her shoulder to steady the swinging lantern.

Taking a deep breath, Sarah began to manipulate the lantern's shutter with her chin and teeth. She blinked rapidly, fighting against the stinging salt spray, as she carefully timed the flashes. Long, short, long – the universal distress signal. She repeated the pattern, praying that someone would see and understand.

The sounds of the fight behind her faded into the background as Sarah concentrated on her task. She knew that every flash could mean the difference between rescue and disaster.

Her muscles ached from the awkward position, but she persevered, driven by the urgent need to summon help.

Between flashes, Sarah's gaze darted towards the shoreline, searching for any sign that her message had been received. The storm made it difficult to see, but she thought she caught a glimpse of movement on the water – perhaps other boats coming to investigate?

Sarah glanced back at the two men still locked in combat.

Ethan's gaze darted around frantically, searching for an escape. In that moment, Sarah saw the decision form in his eyes. A look of reckless abandon crossed his face, and he lunged towards the yacht's wheel.

"No!" Sarah cried out, but her voice was lost in the howling wind.

Ethan grabbed the wheel and wrenched it hard to the side. The yacht lurched violently, nearly vertical as it caught the full force of a massive wave. Sarah's stomach dropped as the world tilted around her. She caught a glimpse of Matthew's horrified expression before the sea rushed up to meet them.

The impact knocked the breath from Sarah's lungs. Icy water engulfed her, the salt stinging her eyes and filling her nose. She thrashed wildly, her bound hands hampering her movements as she fought to reach the surface. The darkness was absolute, broken only by flashes of lightning that illuminated the churning water around her.

Sarah broke the surface, gasping for air. The storm raged overhead, rain lashing her face as she struggled to stay afloat. Debris from the yacht bobbed nearby, the splintered wood a stark reminder of their predicament. She caught sight of Matthew a few yards away, his strong arms cutting through the waves as he searched for her.

"Sarah!" His voice barely carried over the wind, but the fear and desperation in it were clear.

She tried to call back, but a wave crashed over her, sending her under once more. The cold seeped into her bones, her sodden clothes dragging her down. Sarah kicked hard, fighting against the current that threatened to pull her under.

As she surfaced again, Sarah saw a dark shape looming beside her. The overturned hull of the yacht drifted dangerously close, its jagged edges a new threat in the tumultuous sea. She tried to swim away, but her bound hands made it nearly impossible to control her direction.

The waves tossed her about like a rag doll, each one bringing her closer to the wrecked yacht. Fear and exhaustion threatened to overwhelm her. She could hear Matthew calling her name, but the sound seemed to come from everywhere and nowhere at once.

"Matthew!" she cried out, her voice barely audible above the howling wind.

Suddenly, she caught sight of him, lashing out against the choppy waters. Their eyes locked.

Matthew's strong arms sliced through the water with renewed vigour. Sarah could see the strain in his muscles as he fought against the current, refusing to let the sea claim her. She tried to swim towards him, but a wave caught her, sending her tumbling beneath the surface once more.

Panic gripped Sarah as she struggled in the darkness. Her lungs burned, crying out for air. Just as she thought she couldn't hold on any longer, she felt Matthew's hand close around her arm. With a powerful surge, he pulled her up, breaking through the surface of the water.

Sarah coughed and sputtered, gulping in precious air. Matthew's arm wrapped securely around her waist, holding her close as he treaded water. His breath was laboured, but his grip never faltered.

"I've got you," he shouted over the storm, his deep brown eyes meeting hers. "Just hold on, Sarah. I won't let you go."

Sarah did her best to cling to Matthew, her heart pounding

as the waves crashed around them. The icy water sapped her strength, but she refused to give in to despair.

"We need to move away from the wreckage," Matthew shouted over the howling wind. Sarah nodded, understanding the danger of being dashed against the yacht's remains.

With her hands still bound, Sarah knew she couldn't swim effectively. Instead, she focused on keeping her body as streamlined as possible, kicking her legs in sync with Matthew's powerful strokes. The motion helped generate a small amount of warmth, fighting off the numbing cold that threatened to overwhelm her.

Lightning flashed overhead, illuminating Matthew's face. His jaw was set in grim determination, his eyes scanning the turbulent sea for any sign of rescue.

"Matthew," she called out. "I can see a light to the east. It might be the lighthouse!"

Matthew adjusted their course, using Sarah's guidance to navigate through the churning waters. Sarah kept her eyes fixed on the distant flicker, praying it wasn't just a trick of the lightning. She remembered the countless nights she'd spent tending that very light, never imagining she'd one day depend on it for her own survival.

A massive wave rose before them, threatening to separate them. Sarah tightened her grip on Matthew, pressing herself close to his side. "Hold your breath," he warned, just before the wall of water crashed over them.

The world became a swirling chaos of bubbles and darkness. Sarah's lungs burned, but she held on, trusting in Matthew's strength to pull them through. When they finally broke the surface, Sarah gasped for air, coughing up seawater.

"Are you all right?" Matthew asked, concern evident in his voice despite his own laboured breathing.

"Yes," Sarah managed, her voice hoarse but determined. "We can do this, Matthew. I know we can."

A flash of lightning illuminated the chaos around them. Sarah's eyes widened in horror as she saw a large piece of the yacht's debris hurtling towards them, carried by a massive wave. Before she could shout a warning, the jagged wood struck Matthew's shoulder with a sickening thud.

Matthew's cry of pain was lost in the storm, but Sarah felt his body jerk violently. His stroke faltered, and for a heart-stopping moment, they both slipped beneath the surface. Sarah kicked frantically, fighting to keep them afloat as Matthew struggled to regain his rhythm.

When they broke the surface again, Sarah could see the agony etched on Matthew's face. His breathing was laboured, and his movements had slowed considerably. Blood mingled with the saltwater, staining his shirt a dark crimson.

"Matthew!" Sarah shouted, her voice raw with fear and desperation. "Are you all right?"

Matthew gritted his teeth, his eyes meeting hers with unwavering resolve. "I'm fine," he managed, though the strain in his voice betrayed the lie. "Just keep kicking, Sarah. We're going to make it."

"The lighthouse," Sarah gasped, trying to orient herself in the churning sea. "We need to keep moving towards the light."

Matthew nodded, adjusting their course with visible effort. Sarah did her best to assist, kicking her legs in tandem with his strokes, determined to ease his burden in whatever small way she could. She wished desperately that her hands were free, longing to offer more tangible support.

"There! Do you see that?" Matthew shouted, motioning painfully with his head.

Sarah's eyes swept their surroundings, looking for whatever Matthew was pointing out. She couldn't see anything other than raging waves. But then…

"Yes! I see it!"

SALVATION AT SEA

Sarah's heart leapt with hope as she spotted a familiar silhouette cutting through the tumultuous waves. Mr Thorne's boat, guided by his steady hand, approached through the storm. His stormy-grey eyes locked onto Sarah and Matthew.

"Hold on!" Mr Thorne's gruff voice broke through the storm. "We're coming for you!"

Sarah felt a surge of strength at the sight of her mentor. "Did you hear that?" she shouted. "Mr Thorne's here. We're going to be all right! Thank God!"

Matthew managed a weak nod, his face pale with pain and exhaustion. Sarah could see the effort it took for him to keep them both afloat, his injured shoulder clearly hampering his movements.

As the boat drew nearer, Sarah recognised Alexander Davies at Mr Thorne's side. The usually quiet assistant was shouting instructions, his voice barely audible over the crashing waves. Sarah marvelled at the calm efficiency with which the two men worked together, manoeuvring the vessel through the treacherous waters.

"Sarah!" Mr Thorne called out. "We're going to throw you a line. Can you catch it?"

Sarah glanced down at her bound hands, frustration welling up inside her. "My hands are tied!" she shouted back. "Matthew's injured. You'll need to come closer!"

Mr Thorne's eyes narrowed as he took in their predicament. Without hesitation, he steered the boat closer, fighting against the wind and waves. Alexander stood ready at the bow, a rope in his hands.

As they drew alongside, Sarah could see the concern etched on Mr Thorne's face. His eyes met hers, conveying a silent message of reassurance. "We've got you," he said, his voice steady and sure. "Let's get you both out of this water."

Sarah's teeth chattered as the icy water lashed against her face.

As the vessel drew nearer, Sarah could see the boat rock dangerously in the turbulent sea, but Alexander's stance remained steady, his eyes fixed on Sarah and Matthew.

"Hold on!" Mr Thorne's gruff voice carried over the howling wind. "We're almost there!"

Sarah could feel the fight leaving Matthew's body. His injured shoulder had taken its toll, and she could sense him slipping beneath the waves. "Stay with me," she pleaded.

The boat drew alongside them, and Alexander reached out with strong arms. Sarah marvelled at his strength as he effortlessly lifted her from the churning sea. She gasped as the cold air hit her soaked skin, her lungs burning as she gulped in great breaths.

No sooner had her feet touched the deck than Alexander was reaching for Matthew. Mr Thorne's expert handling of the boat kept them steady as Alexander hauled the injured fisherman aboard.

Sarah collapsed against the side of the boat, her chest heaving. She looked up at Mr Thorne, his face a picture of concentration as he navigated the treacherous waters. Decades of experience were evident in every move he made, every adjustment of the tiller.

Gratitude washed over Sarah as she took in the determined faces of her rescuers. Alexander, usually so reserved, now moved with purpose as he tended to Matthew.

"Mr Blackwood's out there too!" Sarah shouted at Mr Thorne. He nodded, signalling he heard, and Alexander deftly stood back up to survey the waves.

Sarah watched as Mr Thorne and Alexander hauled Ethan's waterlogged form onto the boat. His once-immaculate attire now clung to him like a second skin, his hair plastered to his forehead. Despite his bedraggled appearance, Ethan's eyes still held a spark of defiance.

As Alexander secured Ethan's bonds, Sarah couldn't help but feel a twinge of anger. The man she had thought was her friend now sat before her as a criminal.

Ethan's gaze met hers, and Sarah saw no remorse in him. His lips curled into a sardonic smile, as if daring her to judge him.

"Well, Miss Campbell," Ethan said, his voice hoarse from the saltwater. "It seems you've won this round."

"This isn't a game, Ethan. People's lives are at stake." Sarah reprimanded.

Mr Thorne's gruff voice cut through the tension. "Save your breath, Sarah. Men like him don't change their spots."

As the boat turned towards shore, Sarah observed Ethan's demeanour. He sat straight-backed despite his bonds, his chin lifted in defiance. It was clear that even in defeat, he refused to show weakness.

All that had transpired settled on Sarah's shoulders. She glanced at Matthew, who was being tended to by Alexander, then back at Ethan. The contrast between the two men couldn't have been starker.

RETURN TO SHORE

✥

Sarah's legs trembled as she stepped onto the pebbled shore of Weymouth, her sodden dress clinging to her frame. The wind whipped her auburn hair across her face, but she barely noticed, her eyes fixed on Matthew as he was carefully helped from the boat by Alexander and Mr Thorne.

A crowd had gathered on the beach, drawn by the commotion of their dramatic rescue. Sarah recognised familiar faces among them – Mrs Hawkins from the market, young Bill the fishmonger's son, and old Bessie who sold flowers on the Esplanade. Their expressions were a mix of concern and curiosity.

"Someone fetch Dr. Winters!" a voice called out from the throng. Sarah silently thanked whoever had the presence of mind to summon medical help.

As Matthew was laid gently on the sand, Sarah dropped to her knees beside him, her heart clenching at the sight of his pale face and the angry red gash on his shoulder. She reached out, her fingers brushing his cheek.

"Matthew," she whispered, her voice hoarse from the salt water. "Stay with me."

His eyes fluttered open, meeting hers. Despite the pain etched on his features, a small smile tugged at his lips. "Not going anywhere, Sarah," he murmured.

The crowd parted as Dr. Winters arrived, his black bag in hand. He knelt beside Matthew, his experienced hands already probing the wound.

"Miss Campbell," the doctor said, glancing up at her. "You should get yourself seen to as well."

Sarah shook her head, her eyes never leaving Matthew's face. "I'm fine, Dr. Winters. Please, just help Matthew."

As the doctor worked, Sarah became aware of the hushed whispers around her. She caught snippets of conversation – talk of shipwrecks, smugglers, and danger at sea. She knew there would be questions, explanations needed, but for now, all that mattered was Matthew's well-being.

Sarah watched as two constables approached, their faces grim with determination. They flanked Ethan, who stood dripping and dishevelled on the beach, his once-impeccable appearance now as tattered as his schemes. His eyes darted about like those of a cornered animal.

As they clasped irons around Ethan's wrists, a strange mix of emotions washed over her. Relief, certainly, that the truth was finally coming to light. But there was also a twinge of sadness for the man she thought she'd known.

Ethan's gaze locked with hers for a moment as the constables led him away. She saw a flicker of something in his eyes – regret, perhaps? Or just the realization that his carefully constructed facade had crumbled to nothing?

"Good riddance," a voice muttered from the crowd. It was Margery Black, her fiery red hair whipping in the wind as she glared at Ethan's retreating form.

As word spread through the gathering, Sarah could feel the mood shift. Whispers of admiration replaced the earlier shock and confusion. Mrs Hawkins pushed through the throng, her weathered face creased with concern and gratitude.

"Bless you, child," she said, clasping Sarah's hand. "You've saved us all from God knows what."

Others joined in, offering words of thanks and praise. Sarah felt overwhelmed by their appreciation, acutely aware that she was still dripping seawater onto the pebbled beach.

"It wasn't just me," she said, her voice hoarse. "Matthew, Mr Thorne, Arthur – we all worked together."

As if summoned by her words, Mr Thorne appeared at her side. His usually stern face was softened with pride as he placed a hand on her shoulder.

"We saw your signal, you did well, Sarah," he said quietly. "Your parents would be proud."

THE AFTERMATH

Sarah stood on the steps of the Weymouth Town Hall, her heart racing as she watched the proceedings unfold. The past few days had been a whirlwind of activity, with constables swarming through the town and arrests being made left and right.

Reginald Hargrave, the man behind it all, was led out in chains, his once-proud demeanour now shattered. Sarah couldn't help but feel a mixture of satisfaction and pity as she watched him being escorted to the waiting police wagon.

Close behind him came Beatrice Wentworth, her usually impeccable appearance now dishevelled. Jonathan Leighton followed, his naval uniform stripped of its medals. And then, to Sarah's continued disbelief, Reverend Edward Collins, his clerical collar a stark contrast to the handcuffs around his wrists.

"I can't believe how deep this went," Mr Thorne muttered beside her.

Sarah nodded, her throat tight with emotion. "It's like pulling up a weed and finding the roots go halfway across the garden."

"The authorities are still finding some of the caches of smuggled goods, all over the country. Seems as soon as the crashes happened, they sent the goods to the highest bidders, where ever they may be. Who knows if they'll find them all." Mr Thorne said.

"But at least there won't be anymore." Sarah said. "And no more men will die in the wrecks they created."

"Vile work." Mr Thorne almost spat. "Getting men aboard to sabotage the ships! And having more on the shores... such an operation!"

Jonathan Leighton had been the first to break, and had laid out how the shipwrecks had been orchestrated to the courtroom. They had made sure to get men for their cause on the ships themselves, and with the help and communication of those on shore – that had explained the mysterious flashing lights – they were able to ground the ships, and grab the smuggled goods before anyone could notice.

Sarah shuddered at the memory of the prosecutor asking Mr Leighton about inevitable casualties that must have occurred with the wrecks. He had simply shrugged.

As Ethan was brought out, Sarah felt a pang of regret for the friendship she thought they'd shared. He didn't meet Sarah's gaze, as he was pushed into the wagon.

The crowd that had gathered erupted into cheers as the wagon pulled away. Sarah heard her name being called out, along with Matthew's, words of praise and gratitude echoing through the square.

"Three cheers for Sarah and Matthew!" someone shouted, and the crowd took up the cry.

Sarah's cheeks flushed with embarrassment and pride.

Amidst the jubilation, Sarah spotted Arthur Finch standing nervously to one side. She made her way over to him.

"Mr Finch," Sarah said warmly, "I hope you know that Matthew and I have spoken to the authorities on your behalf.

They understand that you were an unwitting participant in all this."

Arthur's shoulders sagged with relief. "Thank you, Miss Campbell. I don't know how I can ever repay your kindness."

Sarah smiled at Arthur, touched by his genuine gratitude. "There's no need for repayment, Mr Finch. Your help was invaluable in uncovering the truth."

"Sarah! The mayor wants a word with you," Mrs Havisham said, beckoning her over.

Sarah made her way through the bustling crowd, their cheers still ringing in her ears. She felt a strange mix of pride and humility as she approached the mayor, his portly figure cutting an imposing silhouette against the Town Hall's stone facade.

"Miss Campbell," the mayor beamed, extending his hand. "I must say, Weymouth owes you a great debt of gratitude."

Sarah shook his hand, feeling the weight of his words. "Thank you, sir, but I couldn't have done it without Matthew and Mr Finch. We all played our part."

The mayor nodded, his eyes twinkling. "Indeed, indeed. But it was your keen mind and unwavering determination that brought this conspiracy to light. Tell me, where is young Mr Fletcher? I'd like to extend my thanks to him as well."

Sarah's smile faltered slightly. "He's still in hospital, sir. The doctors are keeping a close eye on him after... well, after everything that happened at sea."

"Ah, yes, of course," the mayor said, his expression softening. "A harrowing ordeal, to be sure. And you're headed there now, I presume?"

Sarah nodded, feeling a sudden urgency to be by Matthew's side. "Yes, sir. I was just about to make my way over."

"Very good, very good," the mayor said, patting her shoulder. "Give him our best wishes for a speedy recovery. Weymouth needs its heroes hale and hearty."

LOVE'S GENTLE TOUCH

*S*arah sat beside Matthew's hospital bed, her hand gently resting on his. The steady rhythm of his breathing was a comforting sound in the quiet room. Sunlight streamed through the window, casting a warm glow on Matthew's face, which was still bruised but healing.

"You know," Sarah said softly, "I never thought I'd spend so much time in a hospital room."

Matthew's eyes fluttered open, a weak smile tugging at his lips. "Sorry to keep you cooped up here."

Sarah shook her head, her auburn hair catching the light. "Don't be silly. There's nowhere else I'd rather be."

As the days passed, Sarah found herself opening up to Matthew in ways she never had before.

One quiet afternoon, as Sarah was adjusting Matthew's pillows, he caught her hand. "Sarah," he said, "I need to tell you something."

Sarah's heart quickened. "What is it?"

Matthew took a deep breath. "I've been thinking a lot about what happened... about us. I know I sprung my feelings on you rather suddenly before, and I'm sorry if that overwhelmed you. But I need you to know that my feelings haven't changed. If anything, they've grown stronger."

A lump formed in Sarah's throat. She thought about Ethan, about the excitement and novelty he had brought into her life. But as she looked at Matthew, she realised that what she felt for him was something entirely different – something deeper and more enduring.

"Matthew," she whispered, "I think I've always loved you. I was just too afraid to admit it to myself."

Matthew's hand tightened around hers, his thumb tracing gentle circles on her skin. "Sarah," he whispered, his voice thick with emotion, "I've dreamed of hearing those words for so long."

A feeling of rightness that she'd never experienced before flooded through Sarah. She leaned closer, drawn to Matthew as if by an invisible force.

"I'm sorry it took me so long to realise," she said, her free hand reaching up to cup his cheek. Matthew leaned into her touch, his eyes never leaving hers.

The air between them seemed to crackle with anticipation. Sarah's gaze flickered to Matthew's lips, and she found herself inching closer.

Matthew's hand moved to the nape of her neck, his fingers tangling in her hair.

Their lips met in a soft, tender kiss. It was gentle at first, a tentative exploration of new territory. But as Sarah melted into Matthew's embrace, the kiss deepened, filled with years of unspoken longing and newfound understanding.

Sarah's heart soared, and she felt as if she were floating. The kiss was nothing like she'd imagined – it was better. It felt like coming home after a long journey, like finding a safe harbour in a storm.

When they finally parted, both breathless and flushed, Sarah rested her forehead against Matthew's. She couldn't help the smile that spread across her face, mirroring the joy she saw in Matthew's eyes.

BUILDING OUR TOMORROW

Sarah felt a newfound lightness in her steps as she walked alongside Matthew along the Esplanade. The sea breeze tousled her hair, and she tucked a stray strand behind her ear, stealing a glance at Matthew. His hand was warm in hers, their fingers intertwined as naturally as if they'd been doing this for years.

"I can hardly believe it," Sarah said, her voice soft with wonder. "After everything we've been through, here we are."

Matthew squeezed her hand gently. "I always knew we'd find our way to each other, Sarah. It just took us a bit of time to get here."

They paused, looking out over the waves. The lighthouse stood tall in the distance, a constant reminder of where their journey had begun. A rush of gratitude passed through Sarah for Mr Thorne and the home he'd given her in her darkest hour.

"You know," Matthew said, turning to face her, "I've been thinking about our future."

Sarah's heart skipped a beat. "Oh?"

Matthew's eyes sparkled with excitement. "What if we moved back into your family's bakery? We could run it together, just like your parents did. It would be a fresh start for both of us."

Sarah's heart skipped a beat. The idea of returning to the bakery had always been a bittersweet thought, laden with memories of her parents. But now, with Matthew by her side, it felt like a chance to honour their legacy while building something new.

"Matthew, that's... that's perfect," she said, her voice thick with emotion. "But what about your dreams at sea? Of being a fisherman to rival your father?"

Matthew looked out over the rolling waves, deep in thought. "In many ways, that feels like the dreams of a boy. But now…" He looked back at Sarah. "I have something so much better. I have you, and the life that we will build together." He leant in and kissed her. She couldn't help but smile as she kissed him back. "And who knows." Matthew grinned. "The sea might call me back one day, just as the lighthouse might you!"

Sarah chuckled. "Very true. Oh! But what about Miss Havisham? She's done so much for the bakery."

Matthew smiled, his expression thoughtful. "We could keep her on as a senior employee. Her experience would be invaluable, and it would be a way to thank her for everything she's done."

Sarah's mind raced with possibilities. The smell of fresh bread, the warmth of the ovens, the chatter of customers – all mingled with visions of a future with Matthew. It felt right, like pieces of a puzzle finally falling into place.

"Yes," Sarah said, her face breaking into a radiant smile. "Let's do it. Let's bring the Campbell bakery back to life."

∽

Sarah stood at the entrance of St. Mary's Church, her heart pounding with anticipation. The spring breeze carried the aroma of blooming flowers, a sweet fragrance that seemed to herald new beginnings. She steadied herself as she gazed at the wooden doors before her.

The church bells chimed, their melodious peals echoing through Weymouth. Sarah felt a gentle squeeze on her arm and turned to see Mr Thorne, his eyes glistening with pride and affection.

"Ready, my dear?" he asked softly.

Sarah nodded, unable to speak past the lump in her throat. As the doors swung open, she was greeted by a sea of familiar faces. The entire town had turned out for the occasion, filling the pews with smiles and excited whispers.

Her eyes found Matthew at the altar, and the world seemed to fade away. He stood tall and handsome in his best suit, his gaze fixed on her with such love and adoration that it took her breath away.

Sarah's steps were steady as she made her way down the aisle, each one bringing her closer to the future she and Matthew had fought so hard to secure. As she reached him, Matthew took her hand, his touch as familiar and comforting as the lighthouse beam that had guided them through so many stormy nights.

The vicar began the ceremony, his words washing over them as Sarah and Matthew lost themselves in each other's eyes. As they exchanged vows, Sarah's mind wandered to the journey that had brought them to this moment.

She remembered the lonely, grief-stricken girl she'd been, watching her childhood slip away as surely as the tide. She thought of Matthew, the boy who'd shared her loss and understood her pain. They'd grown together, their friendship a constant anchor in a world of change and uncertainty.

Sarah gazed into Matthew's eyes, his warm brown irises reflecting the love and devotion she felt in her own heart. The church's stained glass windows cast a kaleidoscope of colors across his face, making the moment feel almost ethereal.

As the vicar continued the ceremony, Sarah's mind drifted to the countless hours she and Matthew had spent together at South Point Lighthouse. She remembered the nights they'd stayed up late, poring over documents and piecing together the mystery that had threatened their beloved Weymouth. Those moments of shared purpose and determination had only strengthened the bond between them.

The scent of lilies and roses filled the air, reminding Sarah of the bouquets her mother used to arrange for special occasions at the bakery. A bittersweet pang of longing tugged at her heart, wishing her parents could be there to witness this joyous day. Yet, she felt their presence in the love that surrounded her, in the familiar faces of the townspeople who had become her extended family.

Sarah's gaze flickered briefly to the congregation. She saw Miss Havisham dabbing at her eyes with a handkerchief, Mr Thorne beaming with fatherly pride, and even old Tom from the harbour grinning toothlessly from the back pew. These were the people who had supported her through the darkest times, who had believed in her when she'd doubted herself.

As the vicar prompted them to exchange rings, Sarah's hand trembled slightly. Matthew's steady grip anchored her, his touch a silent reassurance. The cool metal of the wedding band slid onto her finger, a perfect fit, just like the life they were about to build together.

PART IV
EPILOGUE

1868

THE HEARTBEAT OF WEYMOUTH

Sarah stood atop the Jubilee Clock Tower, her hand resting gently on her swollen belly. The warm summer breeze washed over her as she gazed out over Weymouth Bay. Matthew's strong arm encircled her waist.

The newly erected tower offered a breathtaking view of the town they'd fought so hard to protect. Sarah's eyes traced the familiar coastline, memories washing over her like the tide below. She could almost see the ghosts of their past selves, so unaware of the adventures that lay ahead.

"It's hard to believe how much has changed," Sarah murmured, leaning into Matthew's embrace.

He nodded, his chin resting atop her head. "And yet, some things remain constant."

As if on cue, the beam from South Point Lighthouse swept across the waters, a familiar sight that never failed to stir something deep within Sarah's heart. It was more than just a beacon for ships now; it had become a symbol of their journey, their unwavering commitment to each other and to the town they called home.

Sarah's gaze drifted to the harbour, where fishing boats

bobbed gently in the fading light. She thought of old Tom and the other sailors who'd unwittingly played a part in their investigation. Their lives, too, had been changed by the events of the past year.

The Esplanade bustled with activity even as evening approached. Tourists and locals alike strolled along the promenade, enjoying the last remnants of a glorious summer day. Sarah spotted Miss Havisham closing up the bakery, and her heart swelled with gratitude.

"Do you ever wonder what your parents would think?" Matthew asked softly, his hand joining hers on her belly.

Sarah smiled, feeling the gentle flutter of their child within. "I think they'd be proud," she replied. "Not just of us, but of how the town has come together."

"They most certainly would be. And they'd be so proud of the effect you've had on this town." Matthew said. "They came together when it mattered most, because of you."

Sarah nodded, her throat tight with emotion. She thought of the long nights spent poring over documents, the heart-pounding chases through Weymouth's winding streets, and the moment she'd truly feared all was lost on that storm-tossed yacht. Yet here they stood, stronger for having weathered it all.

The clock tower's chimes rang out, marking the hour. Sarah felt the baby kick, as if in response to the sound. She laughed softly, placing Matthew's hand where their child moved beneath her skin.

"Another Fletcher with perfect timing," she teased, her eyes sparkling as she met her husband's gaze.

Matthew grinned, the same boyish smile that had first captured her heart all those years ago at the summer fair. "Let's hope this one inherits your knack for solving mysteries," he said, "though perhaps with a bit less danger involved."

Sarah's laughter faded into a contented sigh as she turned back to the view. The sun dipped lower, painting the sky in brilliant hues of orange and pink. In the growing twilight, the lighthouse beam grew stronger.

"We should head back," Matthew said gently. "Miss Havisham's bringing over some of those meat pies you've been craving."

Sarah smiled, thinking of the kindly woman who'd become like family. As they made their way down the tower's winding staircase, Sarah paused, one hand on the railing.

"Matthew," she said softly, "I never thought I'd find a home again after losing my parents. But you, this town, our baby... I've found so much more than I ever dreamed possible."

"The Lord is good." Matthew's eyes shone with love and understanding. He took her hand, bringing it to his lips for a tender kiss. "Come on, love," he said. "Let's go home."

Hand in hand, they stepped out into the bustling streets of Weymouth, ready to face whatever adventures lay ahead – together.

THE FIRST CHAPTER OF 'THE WORKHOUSE ORPHAN RIVALS'

Charlotte Ripley giggled as she scampered down the cobblestone streets, her pigtails bouncing with each step. The warm summer sun cast a golden glow over the bustling city, and the air was thick with the aromas of fresh bread and chimney smoke.

"Wait for me!" called a voice from behind her.

Charlotte spun around, her hazel eyes sparkling, as Lucas Alcott rounded the corner. His cheeks were flushed and he doubled over, panting.

"You're too fast, Charlie," he said, using the nickname that only he was allowed to call her.

Charlotte grinned, not the least bit apologetic. "You'll have to keep up then, won't you?"

Lucas straightened, a playful gleam in his eyes. "Oh, I'll keep up all right." With that, he took off after her, his feet pounding against the uneven stones.

A squeal of delight escaped Charlotte as she fled, weaving through the throngs of people going about their daily business. Vendors hawked their wares, horses whickered, and the general cacophony of the city surrounded them, but in that moment, it was just the two of them, lost in their childish game of chase.

Finally, Charlotte ducked into a narrow alleyway, pressing her back against the cool brick as Lucas skidded to a halt in front of her.

"I caught you," Lucas panted, leaning against the opposite wall.

"For now," Charlotte countered, her eyes twinkling. "But you'll never catch me for good."

Lucas smiled. "You'll never get rid of me, Charlie."

"Over here!" Lucas hissed, gesturing towards a small nook between two buildings. Charlotte followed him, her heart pounding with excitement at the prospect of a new discovery.

Tucked away in the shadows was an old wooden crate, its contents spilling out onto the ground. Lucas knelt down, sifting through the debris with eager hands.

"Look at this!" he exclaimed, holding up a tarnished pocket watch. Its face was cracked, but the intricate engravings along the side still caught the light.

Charlotte gasped, taking the watch gingerly in her hands. "It's beautiful," she breathed, running her fingers over the delicate etchings.

Lucas grinned. "It's yours, then. It's definitely some great treasure. I'm sure it's got all sorts of mysterious hidden away in it. We'll just have to work them out."

Warmth blossomed in Charlotte as she clutched the watch to her heart. This was why she loved Lucas so dearly – he always knew how to make her feel special, like she was the most important person in his world.

Their adventures continued, each day a new escapade. One afternoon found them perched high in the branches of a gnarled oak tree, swapping stories and dreams as the leaves whispered secrets around them.

"When I'm grown," Lucas declared, "I'm going to sail the seas and see the whole world."

Charlotte wrinkled her nose. "The whole world? What about me?"

"Of course you'll come too," he said matter-of-factly. "We'll have grand adventures together, you and I. We'll never be apart."

Charlotte smiled, comforted by the promise in his words.

Then there were the days spent racing through the streets, their shouts of laughter carrying on the warm breeze. Tag was their favourite game, a whirlwind of darting bodies and breathless taunts.

These were the moments Charlotte cherished, the memories she knew she would hold dear for the rest of her life. In those carefree days of childhood, with Lucas by her side, she felt invincible, as though nothing could ever tarnish the innocence of their bond.

CHARLOTTE WATCHED her parents with admiration as they prepared for their day's work. Even at her young age, she understood the sacrifices they made to provide a stable home for her.

Robert Ripley rose before the sun, his movements quiet yet purposeful as he dressed for the docks. Charlotte heard the creak of the wooden floors as he laced up his heavy boots. When he emerged from the bedroom, his face was etched with determination, a man ready to tackle another gruelling day of labor.

"Off to earn our bread, little one," he said, ruffling Charlotte's hair affectionately. Despite the early hour, his eyes crinkled with a warm smile.

Charlotte nodded solemnly. "Be safe, Papa."

With a final nod, Robert strode out the door. Charlotte knew the docks were an unforgiving place, the work arduous and unrelenting, but her father embraced it without complaint. He was a man of quiet strength, unwavering in his commitment to provide for his family.

As the front door closed behind Robert, Jane emerged from the kitchen, her hands already busy tying the strings of her apron. "Good morning, my darling," she said, pressing a kiss to Charlotte's forehead. "Did you sleep well?"

Charlotte nodded, though truthfully, she had been awake for some time, lying in bed and listening to the familiar sounds of her parents' morning routine. It was a comforting ritual, one that anchored her in a sense of security and love.

Jane headed back into the kitchen, bustled around packing her midwife's bag with the necessary tools and supplies. Her movements were efficient yet gentle, a testament to the care she brought to her work. Charlotte knew that her mother's calling was more than just a job – it was a sacred duty, one she embraced with all her heart.

"A new babe is coming into the world today," Jane said, her eyes shining with anticipation. "Isn't that a wondrous thing?"

Charlotte nodded again, her heart swelling with pride. Her mother was a beacon of strength and compassion, a guiding light for those in need.

As Jane gathered the last of her things, she paused to smooth Charlotte's unruly curls. "Mind the house for me, won't you, love? I'll be back before you know it."

With a final kiss and a whispered "I love you," Jane swept out the door, her steps purposeful and her head held high.

Charlotte watched her parents go, their paths diverging into the bustling streets of London, and felt a profound sense of gratitude. Though their work was humble, their dedication knew no bounds. It was through their unwavering efforts that Charlotte's world remained secure, a haven of love and stability in an ever-changing city.

∽

CHARLOTTE'S FEET carried her down the familiar path, her steps light and carefree as she made her way to Lucas's home. The warm summer breeze tousled her hair, and she couldn't help but skip a little, filled with the boundless energy of youth.

As she rounded the corner, the modest dwelling came into view – a humble abode, but one that radiated a sense of comfort and familiarity. Charlotte could already picture Lucas waiting for her, his face alight with that infectious grin that never failed to make her heart swell.

She rapped her knuckles against the weathered door, the sound echoing within the stillness of the narrow street. A gruff voice called out, bidding her entry, and Charlotte slipped inside.

The interior was simple but well-kept, a reflection of the hardworking man who presided over the household. Charles Alcott sat hunched at the small dining table, his broad shoulders straining against the fabric of his shirt as he pored over a tattered ledger. Even in repose, his frame exuded a rugged strength, forged by years of toiling at the docks.

"Mornin', Miss Ripley," he greeted, his voice a deep rumble.

He glanced up, and Charlotte was struck by the intensity of his gaze, those piercing blue eyes that mirrored Lucas's own.

"Good morning, Mr Alcott," she replied, dipping into a polite curtsy.

Charles waved a calloused hand, dismissing the formality. "None of that, now. You're like family 'round these parts." A ghost of a smile tugged at his mouth, softening the harsh lines of his weathered visage.

Charlotte lips curved upwards in response, her heart warmed by the gruff affection he so freely offered. Despite his rough exterior, there was an undeniable tenderness in the way Charles regarded her, a silent acknowledgment of the bond she shared with his son.

As if summoned by her thoughts, Lucas emerged from the back room, his face lighting up at the sight of her. "Charlie!"

Charles's expression shifted, his features melting into an unguarded display of love and pride as he watched his son approach. In that moment, Charlotte glimpsed the depths of his affection, a love so profound that it seemed to eclipse the lingering sorrow that clung to him like a shroud.

For she knew, beneath the gruff exterior and calloused hands, Charles Alcott carried a wound that had never truly healed – the loss of his beloved wife during the very act of bringing their son into the world. It was a pain that had shaped him, hardening his resolve to be both mother and father to the boy who was now his entire world.

And as Lucas threw his arms around his father in a fierce embrace, Charlotte saw it all – the love, the grief, the unwavering devotion that bound this small family together. It was a poignant reminder that even in the humblest of circumstances, the human spirit would shine through, a beacon of resilience and hope in the face of adversity.

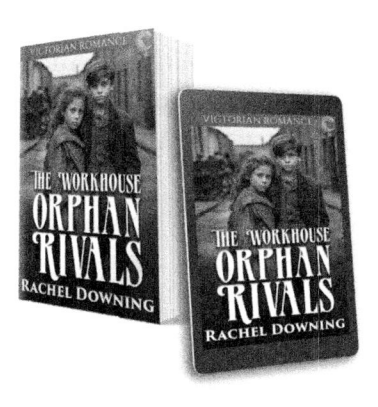

**Click here to read the rest of
The Workhouse Orphan Rivals'**

Childhood sweethearts torn apart. A promise broken. A love that refuses to die.

In the gritty underbelly of Victorian London, Charlotte Ripley's dreams are shattered when her childhood love, Lucas Alcott, chooses ambition over their bond. Thrust into the very workhouses she once feared, Charlotte fights to survive—never expecting to see Lucas again.

But fate has other plans.

When Lucas reappears as her new foreman, old feelings reignite amidst a powder keg of resentment and desire. Can Charlotte forgive the boy who broke her heart? Or will the dashing footman Brandon Johnson sweep her off her feet in her new life as a maid?

As secrets unravel and danger lurks in the shadows, Charlotte must decide who to trust—and who truly deserves her heart.

From workhouse grime to aristocratic shine, this gripping

tale of love, betrayal, and redemption will keep you turning pages long into the night. Watch as childhood promises collide with adult realities, testing the limits of forgiveness and the power of true love.

'The Workhouse Orphan Rivals'

OUR GIFT TO YOU

AS A WAY TO SAY THANK YOU WE WOULD LOVE TO SEND YOU THIS BEAUTIFUL STORY FREE OF CHARGE.

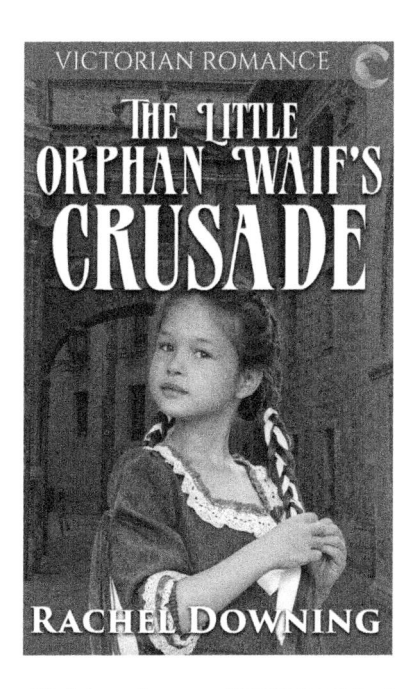

Click here for your FREE COPY of

'The Little Orphan Waif's Crusade'

CornerstoneTales.com/sign-up

In the wake of her father's passing, seven-year-old Matilda is determined to heal her sister Effie's shattered spirit.

Desperate to restore joy to Effie's life, Matilda embarks on a daring quest, aided by the gentle-hearted postman, Philip. Together, they weave a plan to ignite the flame of love in Effie's heart once more.

At Cornerstone Tales we publish books you can trust. Great tales without sex or swearing, but with all of the mystery and romance you expect from a great story.

Be the first to know when we release new books, take part in our fun competitions, and get surprise free books in your inbox by signing up to our free VIP Reader list.

As a thank you you'll receive a copy of 'The Little Orphan Waif's Crusade' straight away, alongside other gifts.

Click here to sign up for our mailing list, and receive your FREE stories.

CornerstoneTales.com/sign-up

LOVE VICTORIAN ROMANCE?

Other Rachel Downing Books

Two Steadfast Orphan's Dreams

Follow the stories of Isabella and Ada as they overcome all odds and find love.

Get 'Two Steadfast Orphan's Dreams' Here!

The Lost Orphans of Dark Streets

Follow the stories of Elizabeth and Molly as they negotiate the dangerous slums and find their place in the world.

Get 'The Lost Orphans of Dark Streets' Here!

The Orphan Prodigy's Stolen Tale

When ten-year-old Isabella Farmerson's world shatters with the tragic loss of her parents, she's thrust into a life of hardship and uncertainty.

Get 'The Orphan Prodigy's Stolen Tale' Here!

The Workhouse Orphan Rivals

Childhood sweethearts torn apart. A promise broken. A love that refuses to die.

Get 'The Workhouse Orphan Rivals' Here!

And from our other Victorian Romance Author Dorothy Wellings…

The Moral Maid's Unjust Trial

Matilda must fend for herself when her father is wrongfully accused for a crime he didn't commit.

Get 'The Moral Maid's Unjust Trial' Here!

If you enjoyed this story, sign up to our mailing list to be the first to hear about our new releases and any sales and deals we have.

We also want to offer you a Victorian Romance novella - 'The Little Orphan Waif's Crusade' - absolutely free!

Click here to sign up for our mailing list, and receive your FREE stories.

CornerstoneTales.com/sign-up

Printed in Great Britain
by Amazon